ENCORE ECHOES

MAGNOLIA KEY
BOOK TWO

KAY CORRELL

ZURA LU PUBLISHING LLC

Published by Zura Lu Publishing LLC

ABOUT THIS BOOK

Tori Duran seeks refuge on the quiet island of Magnolia Key, hiding her past and her identity. She sets her sights on restoring the cherished local theater - a decision that unexpectedly causes her to work side-by-side with Gavin, the gruff owner of the island's bike shop.

Though neither wants the collaboration, as Tori and Gavin work together to breathe new life into the theater, a grudging admiration for each other develops, along with a few undeniable sparks.

But Tori's stubborn resistance to come clean about her past threatens to derail their budding relationship.

When Tori's secret identity is ultimately revealed, it not only jeopardizes her connection with Gavin but also shatters the trust of the entire close-knit community.

With the theater's grand opening quickly approaching, Tori must decide whether to continue fighting for acceptance or start anew somewhere she can keep her past a secret.

Encore Echoes is a captivating story of second chances, the power of community, and the courage to follow your heart - no matter the cost.

This story is dedicated to all those who love the theater, as well as the actors and all who work in the theater. My mother instilled in me a love for live theater and it spilled over into this story.

KAY'S BOOKS

Find more information on all my books at
kaycorrell.com
Buy direct from Kay's Shop at
shop.kaycorrell.com

COMFORT CROSSING ~ THE SERIES

The Wedding in the Grove - (a crossover short story between series - with Josephine and Paul from The Letter.)

LIGHTHOUSE POINT ~ THE SERIES

Wish Upon a Shell - Book One

Wedding on the Beach - Book Two

Love at the Lighthouse - Book Three

Cottage near the Point - Book Four

Return to the Island - Book Five

Bungalow by the Bay - Book Six

Christmas Comes to Lighthouse Point - Book Seven

CHARMING INN ~ Return to Lighthouse Point

One Simple Wish - Book One

Two of a Kind - Book Two

Three Little Things - Book Three

Four Short Weeks - Book Four

Five Years or So - Book Five

Six Hours Away - Book Six

Charming Christmas - Book Seven

SWEET RIVER ~ THE SERIES

A Dream to Believe in - Book One

A Memory to Cherish - Book Two

A Song to Remember - Book Three
A Time to Forgive - Book Four
A Summer of Secrets - Book Five
A Moment in the Moonlight - Book Six

MOONBEAM BAY ~ THE SERIES

The Parker Women - Book One
The Parker Cafe - Book Two
A Heather Parker Original - Book Three
The Parker Family Secret - Book Four
Grace Parker's Peach Pie - Book Five
The Perks of Being a Parker - Book Six

BLUE HERON COTTAGES ~ THE SERIES

Memories of the Beach - Book One
Walks along the Shore - Book Two
Bookshop near the Coast - Book Three
Restaurant on the Wharf - Book Four
Lilacs by the Sea - Book Five
Flower Shop on Magnolia - Book Six
Christmas by the Bay - Book Seven
Sea Glass from the Past - Book Eight

MAGNOLIA KEY ~ THE SERIES

Saltwater Sunrise - Book One
Encore Echoes - Book Two

Coastal Candlelight - Book Three
Tidal Treasures - Book Four (Fall 2024)
And more to come!

WIND CHIME BEACH ~ A stand-alone novel

INDIGO BAY ~
Sweet Days by the Bay - Kay's Complete Collection of stories in the Indigo Bay series

Sign up for my newsletter at my website *kaycorrell.com* to make sure you don't miss any new releases or sales.

CHAPTER 1

T ori stared at her reflection in the glass at the airport as the night darkened outside. She hardly recognized herself. But then, that was the point, wasn't it? She glanced around nervously, but so far no one had recognized her.

Her normally vibrant red hair was now a subdued gray. She never imagined she'd ever let herself go gray, but now, here she was. Simple makeup barely highlighted her features. But that, too, was the point.

She glanced at the screen behind the gate agent. Her plane was set for an on-time departure. She pulled out her phone, checking her ticket she'd purchased that clearly showed general boarding, not her normal first class. She couldn't remember the last time she'd flown anything but first class. But she wanted to blend in with the crowd. There hadn't been time to replace her obviously ridiculously expensive luggage or her designer handbag. At least she'd tried to pick out the least conspicuous one in her closet.

She found a simple pair of black slacks and a white blouse in the back of her closet, along with a wool blazer. Nothing like she would have worn before, always acting her part. Flamboyant, expensive outfits. Shoes that cost more than most people made in a week... or a month.

But not anymore. She'd closed the door on her Fifth Avenue apartment and walked away from all of that. And maybe once she left New York, she'd feel even more comfortable and less recognizable.

At least that was the plan.

She glanced at the boarding pass on her phone. Passenger: Victoria Duran. Destination: Sarasota, Florida. Soon she'd board the plane, and about three and a half hours later, she planned on leaving Victoria behind. She would simply be Tori. The childhood name that her grandmother called her.

The ticket agent called for first-class

passengers to board, and she glanced over at them, trying to shove away her jealousy. She waited for her section to be called and slowly wound her way up to the gate agent. The agent smiled mechanically at her as she scanned her ticket. "Enjoy your flight, ma'am."

Victoria—no, *Tori*, she reminded herself—nodded in reply, matching the gate attendant's automatic smile with one of her own.

She slowly followed the line of passengers down the jetway, each step taking her further away from her problems. At least that's what she hoped.

As she entered the plane, she tried to ignore the first-class passengers and their roomy seats. Why had she never appreciated the perks of first class when she'd flown before? When she found her row, the gentleman in the aisle seat stood and helped her swing her bag into the overhead bin, then let her slip into the middle row seat. There, sandwiched between two broad-shouldered men, she settled back for the flight.

The flight attendants walked through the aisle, closing the overhead bins. The speaker crackled, and soon a perky attendant was explaining all the safety procedures.

She closed her eyes, hoping that neither man

would try to strike up a conversation. The engines rumbled to life, and the plane shook as it pulled away from the gate. They taxied out onto the runway and she gripped the armrests as they soared off into the sky. Leaving Victoria Duran firmly in her past.

Tori Duran flew into her new life. Whatever that life turned out to be.

CHAPTER 2

Tori spent the night at a modest hotel in Sarasota. No penthouse suite for her this time. Not even a waterfront room. Just a standard room, hoping to avoid anyone even noticing her. She headed out early the next morning for Magnolia Key in a nondescript gray rental car. How many years had it been since she'd driven a car? Not much need to have one in New York City. She kept her driver's license current though, for the occasional times she rented a car on a trip. But she couldn't remember the last time she'd actually driven.

At the ferry dock, she sat tapping her fingers on the steering wheel while a long line of cars offloaded. Soon the cars in front of her moved, and she followed them onto the ferry.

She parked, locked her car, and then found her way to the stairs. The spiral staircase led her to the top level of the boat where there was a sitting area on the bow. She adjusted her sunglasses carefully. The sunglasses that once had been just a fashion statement but now were a shield from prying eyes.

Soon Magnolia Key became visible in the distance, and excitement fluttered through her. The island grew larger as the ferry chugged through the green-blue water. As they got closer to the island, the water cleared into the brilliant turquoise color she remembered so well. The sun danced off the tops of the waves, sparkling like diamonds. Like the diamonds safely locked in her safe back home, no longer worn to fancy play openings or charity galas.

She pulled in a deep breath of the salty air, letting it wash through her. The vast openness of it all welcomed her, so different from the stifling high-rise buildings surrounding her back home in New York City.

As they approached the landing, she went back down to her car. Rolling off the ferry as her turn came up, she pulled the car onto solid ground. Magnolia Key.

She wasn't sure what she'd expected when

she arrived. No one to greet her. She didn't know a soul on the island. And yet, she was sure this island was just what she needed.

Brightly painted homes lined the street like candy in the sweet shop that had been around the corner from her childhood home. She drove down sun-dappled Main Street, and it mostly looked like what she remembered. Some freshly painted storefronts here, a missing sign there. The same cobblestone sidewalk she remembered was lining the road.

Her stomach growled as she pulled into a parking space on a side street. She looked in the rearview mirror, once again surprised by the gray hair. How long would it take her to get used to it? She had no reason to create an illusion of herself anymore. She was simply… Tori.

She resolutely slipped out and walked down the street, spying a coffee shop near the boardwalk. How she'd loved that boardwalk. The memories brought a smile to her lips. Long walks along it with her grandmother to indulge in a daily ice cream cone. Fried funnel cakes sprinkled with powdered sugar. And eating at Sharky's with delicious fried *everything*.

She headed over to Coastal Coffee and went

inside. The aroma of freshly brewed coffee and the low hum of conversation welcomed her.

A friendly woman bustled up to her, balancing a tray on one hip. "Welcome to Coastal Coffee. Be with you in a sec. Take any table you'd like."

She took a table near the back and settled onto a worn wooden chair.

The woman approached again. "Hi, I'm Beverly. Coffee?"

She nodded, and Beverly poured her a cup.

"Cream or sugar?"

"Just black."

Beverly motioned to the chalkboard across the room. "That's what we've got today. We're out of the blueberry muffins, but we've got the rest. Or you can get lunch. The chicken salad is good."

"I think I'll just have a chef's salad."

"Coming right up." Beverly hurried away and Tori leaned back in her chair, glancing around the cafe. Only a few other customers were here mid-morning, which suited her just fine.

Beverly returned with her salad and set it in front of her. "First trip to the island?"

"Ah, no. I came here in the summers when I

was a young girl. Haven't been back in… well, a lot of years." She gave a wry smile. "Been quite a few years since I was a young girl."

"Oh, family vacations here?"

"Just my grandmother and me." Her grandmother had been gone more than thirty years, but she still missed her. The one person she could always depend on.

"Well, we're glad to have you back." Beverly's welcome was genuine and warm. "Staying long?"

"I'm not exactly sure. Just taking a much-needed break."

"Where are you staying?"

"I'm staying at Bayside B&B for now. Then I want to find a longer-term rental."

"Darlene's place. You'll love it there." Beverly waved to a couple coming into the cafe, then turned back to her. "Let me know if you want anything else."

She slowly picked at her salad. Her hunger had vanished when she realized the enormity of her decision. Coming to a place where she knew no one. Doing everything for herself instead of the constant help of her assistant. Though her assistant had booked the B&B and made the flight reservation and the car reservation.

Loneliness swirled around her even though she was sitting in the middle of the coffee shop. Though, as far as she could tell, it was her, four other customers, and Beverly. The coffee shops near her apartment in New York City were crammed full of customers at all hours of the day and night. This was a welcome change. Okay, it *probably* was. It would take a bit of time to adjust to this new lifestyle.

She squared her shoulders and took another bite of the salad. She'd faced a lot in the last few months. She could certainly learn to handle this change.

She finished her meal, paid her bill, and headed toward the door. It burst open, and she ran smack into a man's broad, hard chest. The unexpected collision caused a jolt of surprise to ricochet through her.

"Excuse me, ma'am," he said gruffly.

"It's okay." She stepped back. *Ma'am.* She was getting so many ma'ams since she allowed herself to go gray. She self-consciously tucked her hair behind her ear.

He looked closely at her, frowned slightly, then nodded. He slipped past and headed toward an empty table. She stared at him for a moment, wondering if he'd recognized her.

Shaking her head, she headed outside. No one would recognize her like this, would they? Gray hair. Casual clothes—and she needed to get more suitable clothes for here—and far away from the spotlights in New York. A safe place to… to hide.

CHAPTER 3

The next morning Tori woke up slowly, trying to figure out where she was. The quiet was eerily unfamiliar. Ah, yes. The B&B. She slid up and leaned against the fluffy down pillows, enjoying a moment of lazing in bed. Early morning sunlight streamed into her room, illuminating the quaint decor. She climbed out of bed and headed over to the window, looking outside at the bay that stretched between the island and the mainland. Pink hues tinted the clouds over the water. The ferry was approaching the island. She glanced at the clock. Seven. Much earlier than her usual time to get up, but then she hadn't stayed up late into the night like she usually did. There was no need for that now.

She quickly got dressed in a pair of shorts and a simple blouse and went downstairs. The aroma of freshly brewed coffee, baked bread, and a hint of cinnamon led the way. Darlene greeted her as she entered the dining room. "Good morning, Tori. Hope you slept well."

"I did. Well, I admit I ended up turning on a noise app on my phone last night. I wasn't used to how quiet it was here. It's always noisy in New York."

"I bet." Darlene motioned for her to sit and poured her some coffee.

"Just black, thank you." Tori reached for the cup.

"Help yourself to what you want from the sideboard. There's quiche, oatmeal, and cinnamon rolls. Or yogurt and granola if that's more your thing. Oh, and freshly squeezed orange juice."

"Thank you." She went over to the sideboard, her mouth watering. Steam rose from the pot of oatmeal, and the light glaze on the cinnamon rolls tempted her. She self-righteously decided on yogurt and fruit, then with a shrug and a grin, grabbed a cinnamon roll. Why not?

A young couple came in, holding hands,

looking at each other as if there were no other people in the world.

She slid into her seat, trying not to look like she was watching them. She could do that look the young girl had. She'd perfected it once. She could actually do about any expression someone asked of her. The look, the body language. All of it.

But there was a strong connection between the couple. She could almost feel it, see it. Had she ever felt that connected to a person?

"Good morning." Darlene's words interrupted her thoughts, and the couple broke their locked gaze to turn and look at her. "Breakfast is on the sideboard. Coffee?"

"Just coffee. Can we take it out to the beach?" The young man smiled and casually dropped his arm around the woman's shoulders.

"Sure can. Let me get some to-go cups."

Darlene came back with the cups, and the couple disappeared out the door. Darlene turned to her. "They got married here a year ago. They're back to celebrate their first anniversary. Lovely young couple."

"That's nice that they could come back to celebrate."

"I get a lot of repeat guests here. Some

come back year after year. It's nice to get to know them over the years."

"I used to come to the island every summer, too. With my grandmother. I have such fond memories of those days."

"Magnolia has a way of calling people back, again and again." Darlene paused by the table. "Do you mind if I join you? Could really use a cup of coffee myself."

"Yes, please do."

Darlene sat across from her. "So any big plans for the day? Going to go explore around the island some?"

"I plan to. Though, I have to admit, I'm not too fond of driving. Not much chance to drive in New York City. I don't even own a car." And she had a driver back home to take her anywhere she wanted to go, but she didn't mention that.

"It's easy to walk to most places, but if you want you could rent a bike. That's a great way to get around the island."

Her brow creased. How long since she'd ridden a bike? But once you learned how, you could always ride one, right? "That sounds like a plan."

"It's not far from here. It's called... The

Bike Shop." Darlene smiled. "Gavin, the owner, is all about simple and straightforward."

"Then that's what I'll do. I'm looking forward to poking around and seeing what's changed since I came here when I was a girl."

"Well, some things change here in Magnolia, and some things forever stay the same," Darlene said as she rose. "I should get going. Have a handful of guests coming in today and need to make sure their rooms are ready. Let me know if you need anything."

"I'm good. Thanks."

Bike riding. That wasn't something she thought she'd be doing when she decided to come here. But what had she thought she'd be doing? She was used to her hours being filled. Her nights lasting long into the early morning hours. Now her day stretched out before her with nothing really planned. Now *that* was a new experience for her.

Gavin rolled out another bike and set it in front of the shop. A lady's bike in a bright turquoise color. He placed it next to a pink bike. He wasn't really into bike colors—he'd ride anything—but the women sure seemed to like the teal, the pink, and the yellow bikes, so he made sure to have them around.

He'd recently expanded into some electric bikes, although there wasn't much need for them seeing as Magnolia Key was as flat as can be, but a few customers had rented them. He wanted to provide what the customers wanted.

He also had three-wheeled bicycles for those a little unsteady and unsure of the whole biking thing. Plus he'd purchased a handful of tandem bikes and some trailers to pull kids behind the bikes. If there was a market for it, he provided it.

He sucked in a deep breath of the sea air. He'd missed that when he lived in the city. But the city, with all its noise and commotion, had convinced him to move back to Magnolia Key. The island he'd grown up on but swore when he left for college that he'd never return to. And yet. Look at him now. He'd been back almost twenty years, and most days he was sure he'd made the right decision. Most days.

With one last look to make sure he had an enticing array of bikes outside, he headed back into the shop.

He moved behind the counter and shuffled

through invoices. He didn't mind this part of the shop. The business side. And working on the bikes to make sure they were in perfect shape to rent. Unfortunately, he did have to deal with the customers. He never could figure out how a non-people person like him bought a bike shop where dealing with customers was a constant in his job. At least he'd hired some help now. He usually had them deal with the customers.

If the new bridge ever actually got finished, he wondered if his business would grow—or possibly decline. A lot of people took the ferry over and rented bikes for the day. But when they could easily just drive over the bridge, would they even want to rent the bikes? He wasn't big on change and kept hoping the bridge would continue getting delayed.

No use worrying about that now. He couldn't change it.

Jonny, one of his workers, came out from the back of the shop. "Just heard from one of our customers. They have a flat tire. I'm going to run and get the bike so we can fix it. I'll bring them a replacement bike."

"Okay. See you in a bit."

He went back to sorting through the bills.

He startled slightly when he heard a woman's voice. "I'd like to rent a bike."

It was a melodious voice—lyrical, full of emotion. Lyrical? He smirked inwardly at the sudden poetic turn of his thoughts. His high school English teacher would be so proud.

He looked up and smothered his surprise, clenching his jaw. It was the woman who ran into him yesterday at Coastal Coffee. Just what he needed. A customer who couldn't even walk out a door without running into people wanted to rent a bike.

CHAPTER 4

Tori looked at the man behind the counter and tried to hide her surprise. It was the man who had run into her at the coffee shop yesterday. But he didn't act like he recognized her. She shifted uncomfortably at his lack of awareness, not knowing if she should bring it up or not. She decided not bringing it up was the smartest choice.

She swept her gaze around the shop. It was clean and neat, with a faint scent of oil and rubber. Daily and weekly rates were clearly posted behind the counter. The faint sound of a radio drifted out from the back of the shop through a door that said no admittance.

"So, a bike?" she asked again.

"Yes, we rent bikes here," the man said brusquely.

"I need a bike for a few weeks, I imagine."

"You don't know?" His steel-blue eyes narrowed.

"I'm not sure how long I'm staying. Could be a few weeks. Could be longer." Did he want to rent her a bike or not? And was it any of his business that she had no idea how long she was staying? If she was staying? Or why she was even here on Magnolia, for that matter. Everything about his attitude made her bristle.

"Let's go outside and you can choose one." It was more of a command than an ask. He came out from behind the counter and strode toward the door with an obvious sense of purpose.

She followed along behind him, irritated but not knowing if there was another bike shop on the island where she could rent a bike from someone who actually wanted to do business with her.

He stood at the side of the line of bikes, his arms crossed over his chest. His broad shoulders were set in a stance of annoyance. The morning sun lit up the gray streaks in his dark brown hair.

A dark tan highlighted the rugged set of his jaw. He might even be handsome if he weren't so... unapproachable.

"You do know how to ride a bike, don't you?"

"Of course." She bristled. But did she still remember?"

"Want a three-wheeler? They're more steady but a bit harder to navigate around corners."

"No, a regular bike is fine."

He looked at her doubtfully. "Pick one. Try it."

She looked over the array of bikes in bright colors. The sun cast shadow images of them on the pavement. Nervousness swept over her. What if she didn't remember how to ride? What if she fell in front of him? Then anger crept through her at her self-doubt. And why did she have to prove anything to him, anyway?

She grabbed a teal bike with a big basket on the front and wheeled it out to the edge of the street. Climbing on it, she sent a little prayer skyward that she remembered how to ride. She stood on one pedal, pushing it down until the bike started to move. She wobbled a bit as she got started, but thankfully she managed to steer it straight and headed down the block. Her cheeks rose with a goofy grin as she realized she had this. She *could* ride. When she got to the end of the block, she turned around and rode back, her confidence mounting with each rotation of the pedals.

He was still standing there, watching her carefully. Yes, he *might* have been handsome if he wasn't such a grouch.

"See?" She climbed off the bike, proud of herself.

"Good. I don't really like to rent to people who just fancy that they know how to ride."

How did he ever do any business with his grumpy attitude? "I'd like this one if it's available." She felt like she'd made a connection with it. It had proven to him, to her, that she could still ride. She needed all the support she could get these days, even if it came from inanimate objects.

He nodded and headed back inside without another word. He rang her up, still not speaking. "Call if you have any problems. Number is on the receipt." But the words were said automatically, not like he really wanted her to call with any problems.

Finally, he handed her the receipt, and their gaze locked briefly. She snatched the receipt and tucked it in her pocket. "Thank you. Hopefully, I won't have any problems." Because she sure didn't plan on ever calling him for help.

She headed to the door and took one last look back at the surly owner. He was already back sorting through his paperwork without a further glance at her.

Fine. He must be the only rental shop on the island if he still got customers with that attitude of his.

She climbed back on the bike—a bit unsteady at first—and glanced at the window to see if he was watching her. Good. No sign of him. She wobbled down the street a bit until she caught her balance again. See, this wasn't going to be too hard now, was it? A small thrill of independence seeped through her. She could do what she wanted, when she wanted, answering to no one. She reached forward and jangled the bell on the handlebar, a smile slipping onto her lips. The breeze blew her hair and the rhythmic motion of pedaling soothed her nerves. A strong sense of freedom surged through her. This was her life now. Tori's life. And she planned on fully embracing it.

But now she had no idea where she was headed. No real plans. She didn't know anyone. Suddenly, she turned the bike around and headed back to Coastal Coffee. At least she'd met one friendly person there. Beverly. And right now, she could use a friendly smile.

CHAPTER 5

Beverly balanced a tray on one hip as she headed over to Nash's table. "You all good? You're in late today." Nash was always her first customer of the day.

"Yep, had an early morning job I had to get to. Made my own coffee at home. Remind me not to do that again." He grinned up at her, holding up his mug.

She smiled back, poured him more coffee, then turned to hurry toward the kitchen with the tray of dishes she'd cleared.

Her best friend, Maxine, came rushing out of the kitchen. "I think every person on Magnolia has decided to come here to eat today. I've never seen it this busy."

"It is a bit nuts, isn't it?" But Beverly didn't

mind. She loved the busy days, greeting her customers and chatting with them when she had a moment. The clank of dishes and silverware and the intermittent burst of laughter. She'd had no idea when she purchased the tiny cafe all those years ago that she would expand it and it would become such a popular place on the island. Pride flowed through her at her accomplishment as she turned to wait on yet another couple who entered the cafe.

Things finally slowed down later in the morning, and she grabbed her friend for a cup of coffee. "Let's sit."

They sat at the counter sipping coffee but keeping an eye on the handful of customers in case they needed anything. She relaxed as the familiar hum of low conversation and the occasional clink of the coffee cups surrounded them. She turned to Maxine.

"So I heard that the section of beachy decor at Second Finds is growing. Seems like it's a big hit." Beverly took a sip of her coffee, enjoying the flavor of the new coffee beans she'd ordered.

Maxine's eyes lit up. "Dale says at this rate, I'll take over his whole shop." She laughed "As if. But I am having fun. Dale and I are going to make a big run up the state and hit some estate sales, looking for more furniture for him to fix up and me to paint." She scrubbed at a few specks of paint on her hands. "I swear, I never get all the paint off me."

"I'm glad it's working out. You're very talented." Beverly glanced over at the bookcase that Maxine had refinished for a lending library. The whole lending library idea had been a hit too. Her customers were constantly borrowing or donating books to it. She might even have to make room for another bookshelf.

The door opened, and a woman from yesterday returned. The one who had looked a bit lost. She hesitated in the doorway. Beverly rose and waved to her.

"No, don't get up," the woman said. "I just came in for a cup of coffee."

"Would you like to join us?" Beverly offered. No use having her sit alone again. She got the feeling the woman would welcome the company.

"Yes, I would, thank you."

Beverly poured her a cup of coffee and slid it toward her. "I'm sorry, I didn't catch your name yesterday."

"It's... Tori."

"Nice to meet you, Tori. And this is

KAY CORRELL

Maxine." Beverly glanced at Maxine. "Tori used to come here as a girl."

"With my grandmother. Every summer." Tori smiled, a wistful look in her eyes. "I looked forward to it every year. But then, as I got older... well, I thought other things were more important. They weren't, but I was too young to realize it back then."

"We all make crazy choices when we're younger." Maxine's eyes clouded for a moment, then she grinned. "But I'm hoping I'm making better choices now."

"Aren't we all hoping we get smarter as we age?" Beverly nodded and turned to Tori. "So, are you exploring the island today? Seeing what's changed?"

"I'm just starting to. I rented a bike since I'm not big on driving. Got one at The Bike Shop."

"Ah, so did you meet Gavin?"

"Older man? Handsome and grumpy?" Tori gave a wry grin.

"That's our Gavin." Beverly laughed. "He grows on you as you get to know him. But mostly he likes to keep to himself."

"I got that. I thought for a few minutes he was going to refuse to rent a bike to me. And he barely said anything to me while I was at his shop."

"He's a man of few words. But he really is a good man under all that grumpy facade of his."

"I'll have to take your word for it." Tori shook her head.

The door opened again, and Beverly grinned. "Speaking of the devil."

Gavin strode across the floor, not saying hi to anyone, although Beverly was fully aware he knew the customers still sitting at the tables. He headed over to the counter. "Got my to-go order?"

Beverly stood. "Sure do. Let me just grab it for you. Oh, Gavin, you've met Tori, haven't you?"

He just bobbed his head, hardly glancing at Tori. She shook her head as she went into the kitchen. Gavin was his own worst enemy. Keeping up his walls. Afraid to let anyone in. Not that she really blamed him after what had happened. But still, how many years could you hold a grudge against the whole world?

A knot tightened in Tori's stomach, his indifference stinging more than it should. Her heart drummed in irritation. She wasn't sure Gavin could annoy her any more than he had at The Bike Shop, but it appeared he could. He was basically ignoring her. Or was it more... dismissing her? What in the world made him think he could just keep acting like a cold-hearted jerk? Not that she cared. She'd gotten her bike. That's all she needed from him.

Beverly returned and handed Gavin a sack. "Here you go."

"Thanks." Gavin dropped some bills on the counter, turned, and walked briskly to the door, his footsteps ringing with dismissal.

Fine then. He'd hardly acknowledged her. She was fine with that. Really. Okay, not really. She was used to people recognizing her. Wanting to talk to her. Being *nice* to her. But then, she wanted her anonymity now, didn't she?

Yes. Yes, she did. She wanted to fly under the radar in hopes they didn't find her.

And really, why did his opinion of her matter, anyway? It didn't.

"His bark is worse than his bite, I promise."

Beverly's voice was laced with understanding and compassion.

Compassion she herself wasn't willing to show after how he'd treated her. "If you say so."

Maxine set down her coffee and leaned forward. "Did you hear the rumor that someone is interested in buying the old theater and tearing it down?"

"No," Beverly said, her words cutting through the air. "That can't happen. I know it's closed now, but with a bit of work, it could still be used for... something."

"Rumor has it that it might be Miss Eleanor's son, Cliff, wanting to buy it."

Maxine and Beverly passed a look between them, but Tori wasn't sure what that was about.

"Cliff needs to be stopped. Both his desire to build his high rise at the end of the boardwalk and his ridiculous idea to tear down the theater."

"A high rise at the end of the boardwalk?" Tori frowned. "That seems so wrong. It will ruin the whole atmosphere."

"We're trying to stop him." Beverly shook her head. "But Cliff always seems to do just what he wants. What's best for him." Bitterness edged her words.

"I remember the theater from when we used to come here. My grandmother would take me to plays there."

"They used to put on so many plays there. Always had two productions in the summer. And then another couple in January and February when the snowbirds come to hide out from winter. Oh, and the children's Christmas program was held there. The high school graduation. And a few other events during the year. Oh, and movie nights. Can't forget those."

"Right, the movie nights. We went almost every week when we were girls, didn't we?" Maxine's lips curled into a gentle smile, her eyes full of warmth at the memories.

"You two knew each other back then?"

"Best friends. Since—well, since we were born. Maxine just moved back here a bit ago. Love having her back," Beverly said.

She was envious of the close relationship they had. A lifelong friendship. Something she'd never had. She pushed her jealousy away and went back to the theater talk. "Why is it closed now?"

"The repairs got expensive, I guess. I'm not sure who owns it now. It's been sold a few times, but never opened again." Beverly shook her head.

"That's a shame. It was such a pretty theater."

"It was." Maxine stood. "I'll get coffee refills for our remaining customers."

"I should get back to work, too."

"Thanks for letting me join you." Tori was thankful for the company.

"Anytime."

Tori paid for her coffee and rose. "I think I'll go now. I'm ready to poke around town a bit. See what's changed. What's the same."

"Have fun."

"Oh, is Sharky's still here?"

"Sure is."

"Perfect. I think I'll have dinner there tonight." She turned and headed outside to get her bike.

She climbed back on it and was pleased that she didn't wobble nearly as much as she headed out. Many of the storefronts had new stores in them, of course. There was still the park and gazebo just off Main Street. That had been kept up nicely, and it looked like the gazebo was freshly painted. She and Grams used to come and listen to concerts at the park. So many memories.

She pedaled back down the street and ended up putting her bike on a bike rack so she could walk along the sidewalks. She popped into a few stores and made a mental note to come back and buy some clothes that were more appropriate for a stay here on the island.

She made it to almost the end of the Main Street and there it was. The theater. The marquee, once bright and beckoning, stood faded with just a few letters clinging to it. The bright green door had faded to a pale mint color, the paint peeling, proclaiming years of neglect.

She ran her hand along the brick wall, remembering coming here with her grandmother. The excitement of opening night. Grams always liked to come on opening night. She was pretty sure these early trips to the shows were what started her down the path to her career.

She closed her eyes briefly, willing the flashes of memories of her former career to fade. No use dwelling on the past.

She turned and slowly walked around the building, spying a broken window here and the peeling remains of the last show behind a glassed panel there. She peered in through the dusty windows, so sad to see this beautiful building in such disrepair. She could almost feel the excitement and anticipation that used to fill the theater. The hushed tones of conversation as people took their seats. The quiet when the stage lights would snap on.

She walked around the building and tried the back door, not knowing what she would do if it opened, but it was locked. Sadness swept through her at this abandoned theater. No longer considered useful. Left to decay.

She walked back to the front and stood staring at the marquee. How great would it be if the theater could be restored back to its former glory? Become a functioning part of Magnolia again? Become useful. Make a comeback from this shadow of its former self.

A gentle tug at her heart let her know what she wanted to do. What she *had* to do. Or at least she'd try.

CHAPTER 6

L ater that evening, Tori walked down the boardwalk. She'd made some phone calls after talking to Darlene and set her plan in action. But right now she was headed to Sharky's. Her mouth watered in anticipation of her favorite item on their menu. Fried grouper with a side of hush puppies. Her grandmother always let her pick where they would go to eat, and she'd once picked Sharky's five days in a row, ordering the same meal over and over. Her grandmother had finally begged her to choose another restaurant. She smiled at the memory. She just hoped their menu hadn't changed.

She strolled down the boardwalk retracing the exact same steps she'd taken all those years ago. Couples passed her, hand in hand. A young

KAY CORRELL

child danced around his mom as they stood looking out at the water. The salty air blew tufts of her hair this way and that. Contentment drifted through her as she walked along, the familiarity of the scene enveloping her like a hug.

When she walked through Sharky's open door, she smiled. No, nothing had changed. At all. And the scrawled menu behind the bar reassured her that her beloved meal was still on the menu. The rustic charm of the place welcomed her, along with the hum of conversation and the clanking of beer glasses.

A waitress hurried over. "The tables are full right now. You can wait, or you can grab a seat at the bar and eat there."

"The bar is fine." She found an empty barstool and slipped onto it, then turned to say hello to the man sitting next to her and froze. Seriously? Was the town playing tricks on her?

She set her shoulders and pasted on a smile. "Good evening, Gavin. Nice to see you again." As if.

He did his now familiar slight bob of his head, basically dismissing her, and turned back to his beer.

His dismissal made her feel small and

invisible. But…wasn't invisibility what she wanted?

"Can I get you something to drink? Eat?" the bartender asked.

"I'll have the fried grouper with a side of hush puppies. And a beer. That light one you have on tap will be fine." Though she was used to drinking fancy craft beers in bottles.

He handed her a frosty mug with the beer and she took a sip, the cold liquid doing nothing to soothe her annoyance. She set down the glass.

Awkwardness crackled in the inches between her and Gavin. The bartender delivered Gavin's meal—fried grouper and hush puppies. Probably the only thing they'd ever agree on.

She took another sip of her beer and then turned to him in an effort to crack the icy atmosphere and get through his brooding silence. "That's uh… that's my favorite meal here too."

He turned to stare at her for a moment, then went back to his meal without saying a word.

She shouldn't have bothered to even try with the man. Anger flared through her. "Are you always this talkative and friendly?"

41

He set down his fork. "I normally get to eat my meal in peace and quiet."

"Ah, so that gives you the excuse to be so rude."

"Look... lady—"

"Tori." She cocked an eyebrow as she countered him.

He eyed her, not saying a word.

Unwilling to be deterred, she continued. "I just wanted to ask you if you knew much about the theater here in town since I know you grew up here."

He raised an eyebrow. "You know that how?"

"Darlene mentioned it."

"Why were you two talking about me?"

She let out her breath in frustration. "We were talking about your bike shop, not you specifically."

"Why do you want to know about the theater?" He eyed her suspiciously.

"Because I think it's sad that it's gotten so run down. It used to be so... so..." She searched for the right word. "Magnificent. So full of life."

"You saw it when it was open?"

"I did. I came here often with my

grandmother. We always went to opening night at the theater. I so looked forward to those nights. And now... it's shuttered, and it seems like such a waste."

"It is. But there's not really anything you can do about it, now is there?"

"Maybe not. Maybe so." She eyed him defiantly.

Gavin swiveled in his chair to face her, his interest piqued in spite of his desire to be left alone. His curiosity won out. "Like what, exactly?"

She shifted uneasily on her seat, biting her lip. Her eyes showed hesitation, yet behind the hesitation was a determination he found intriguing. Was she some kind of investor determined to reshape the town? Determined to tear things down and put up something new? There was enough of that going around with Cliff Griffin wanting to put up a monstrosity at the end of the boardwalk. Why wouldn't people just leave the town alone? It was fine, just like it was.

"Like... buy it," she finally said.

"And tear it down like Cliff wants to do?"

"No, that should never happen. The theater is a town landmark. Part of its history." Her voice rose with a hint of passion.

Okay, they agreed on that. "But why would you buy it?"

"To restore it. Open it up again. Fill it with stage productions, movie nights, and any other events that could be held in it."

He couldn't miss how her eyes lit up when she talked about it. She seemed sincere, but her plan puzzled him. "But why would you want to do that? You don't even live here."

"I think the theater deserves that much, doesn't it? And… I'm thinking of moving here. At least long enough to get the theater up and running."

"You're going to move here and renovate the theater?" He was still trying to wrap his head around her plan. And why she was doing it.

"If I can come to terms with the owner, yes. Darlene was making some calls to see if she could find out who owned it now. And I peeked in the windows, but I'd need to get inside to get a better idea of how much work needs to be done."

"So you hatched this plan without even going inside and seeing the property?" He couldn't hide his disbelief.

Her eyes flashed. "Yes, I did. I said it was a plan. And yes, I need more information. I'm just trying to… to help. Get it back up and running. What's wrong with that?"

"Nothing's wrong with it, lady—Tori—it just seems like it's a half-baked plan, is all."

"So you'd rather see the building just rot away until it can't be saved?"

"No, of course not." Why was she twisting his words?

The bartender arrived with her order, and she held up a hand. "I'm sorry. Could I get that to go, please?" Her tone was brisk and clearly showed her irritation.

She paid her bill and slid off her barstool. Gavin felt an inexplicable urge to stop her.

"I didn't mean to run you off—"

"Didn't you?" she countered, her eyes betraying a hint of hurt. "Have a nice evening."

She turned and hurried out the door.

Guilt poked at him that he'd annoyed her enough to make her leave, but he could at least finish his meal in peace now. But somehow, that thought didn't comfort him.

The guilt jabbed at him again as he stared at the empty stool beside him.

Because really, wouldn't he like the theater to be opened again? Not that he'd get involved with it. He'd seen firsthand what happened when he tried to help out the town with one of its projects. He wasn't going to let that happen again. Especially with a woman with a half-baked plan and a surprising sense of conviction.

The brisk walk back to Darlene's B&B did little to quell the storm of emotions rolling through Tori. Gavin's words echoed in her mind, mingling with frustration and the reluctant knowledge, infuriatingly, that his words held a bit of truth. The man was impossible. And rude. And just maybe exasperatingly right about her plan. She hadn't even seen the inside very well. Just stolen a few quick glances. Why had she decided that buying it would be a good idea?

Only... she wanted to. She wanted to breathe life back into it. Let other people experience the joy she used to feel when she went to a play there. Maybe if she did this for the town, maybe then... who knows? Maybe she'd feel like she was paying back for the mistake she'd unknowingly made back home. And New York held no appeal for her now. Not with the wheeling and dealing in the industry. Not with the noise and crowds.

Maybe she could settle down here in Magnolia.

She stepped into the B&B, its warmth and coziness in sharp contrast to her encounter with Gavin.

"Oh, back so soon?" Darlene's voice held a blend of surprise and concern.

She managed a half-smile. "I... um... I decided to get my dinner to go."

"I'm glad you're back. I did find out a little bit about the theater. The strange thing is, it was just purchased a month or so ago. I hadn't heard that."

"So it's not for sale?" Her heart sank. All her plans crumbled into fine grains of sand.

"That's another strange thing. It is for sale. Again."

"I don't understand." She tried to piece together the puzzle.

"I don't either, but I arranged for you to pick up the key from the Realtor's office in the morning. He said you could look around inside.

He's going to be on the mainland, but his secretary will give you the key."

"That's great. I can't wait to see it. Though I wonder why someone would buy it and then list it right away?"

"I'm not sure either." Darlene shook her head.

"Thank you for finding out all of that for me."

"Ah, don't thank me. If you could really purchase it and get it opened again, it would mean the world to me. I have so many memories of times spent there. I hate to see it just deteriorate like it has."

"Well, tomorrow I'll give it a look. See if I think it can be restored." Her hopes rose again as she climbed the stairs to her room. The thought of restoring the theater and giving back to this town that had given her so many wonderful memories reignited her determination. She sat at a small table in her room and spread out her dinner, still a bit annoyed that she hadn't been able to eat it fresh out of the frier at Sharky's. But she couldn't bear to spend another minute talking to that insufferable man. If she never had to talk to Gavin again, it would be too soon.

As she ate her meal alone, his words and his dismissive attitude lingered in her mind, a persistent annoyance. Aggravated—at him, at herself—she got up from the table and looked out the window, her mind full of plans for the theater and the unsettling thoughts of the man who had unwittingly stirred her determination even further.

CHAPTER 7

The next morning, Tori stood in front of the grand, aged facade of the theater with a mix of excitement, anticipation, and apprehension. What would she find when she went inside?

She slid the key into the lock on the front door and turned the key. The lock didn't budge. She pushed on the door, tried again, then pulled on the handle. Frustration surged through her. So close.

She took the key out, glared at it, then slipped it in the lock again. The lock clicked open without a problem and the door swung open. A smile broke across her face. Yes. Success. She was finally going to see the inside.

She stepped across the threshold into the

lobby. The musty smell mixed with echoes of laughter and conversations from long ago. She blinked as it took a few moments for her eyes to adjust to the dimly lit lobby.

She walked past the ticket counter and ran her gaze over a line of peeling posters. The last shows before the theater had closed. A play. A movie marathon night. A performance by the high school choir. Each one a decaying fragment of the theater's once-vibrant past. She traced a finger over the poster for the stage play, feeling a connection to it and the actors who'd played their roles.

She turned, walked across the slanted floor of the lobby, and pushed open the swinging door to the actual theater. Rows of seats stretched before her. The lower level was split into three sections. She turned around to see the upper tier, her favorite place to sit. First row of the upper tier.

Memories swirled around her as she climbed the stairs. She walked down the front row and sat in her favorite seat, placing her hands on the wooden railing. She could almost feel her grandmother's presence. She actually turned to the seat beside her, half expecting to see her grandmother reading through the show's program. Closing her eyes, she let the memories engulf her. She could almost feel the pulse of the theater, the noise of the crowd settling into their seats, the anticipation.

After a few minutes, she finally pushed up off the seat and went down to the main level to poke around. In a side office, she flicked some of the light switches. When she walked back into the theater, the huge chandelier hanging from the center of the ceiling cast sparkling, magical light across everything. She clapped her hands in excitement.

She forced herself to walk right past the stage and headed to the backstage area. With the flip of another switch, bare bulbs harshly illuminated the area.

Old props were stacked in the far corner. A dressing table with a mirror lined with lights stood on one side of the room. A few doors on the left led to what must have been dressing areas.

She trudged around the area, picking up a pair of black pumps and flipping them over. Tap shoes, now silent, the metal taps dull from use. She set them down and picked up a floral scarf, shaking the dust off it. The dust floated in the light of the bare bulbs. This prop, once a piece of a costume in one of the plays, now just a faded piece of cloth. She carefully folded it up and set it aside, wondering which actress had worn it and which plays it had been part of.

One wall was lined with clothing racks that were still filled with costumes. Running her fingers over a silk dress that looked like it was from the 1920s, she closed her eyes, imagining an actress wearing it, the spotlights on her as she moved across the stage with the audience following her every move, listening to her every word.

She stepped away from the costumes and turned her gaze upward to the ceiling, eyeing it carefully. She saw no sign of water damage, which was good. But she'd have to have a contractor look it over if she was serious about buying and renovating it.

She was serious, wasn't she? It couldn't replace what she'd lost... but at least it would give her life some meaning again.

She finally walked back out into the main theater and stared at the stage. She could no longer ignore it. She climbed up on it as familiar feelings crept over her.

Her footsteps echoed as she crossed the worn floorboards. She turned to face the chairs, the audience, and could almost hear their applause. A sound that she hadn't heard in months and months. Not since her last performance on Broadway, a box office smash that had broken all records of ticket sales.

The perfect life… until it wasn't.

CHAPTER 8

Tori headed over to Coastal Coffee the next morning. Darlene was busy today with an inn full of guests and too preoccupied to chat, leaving Tori craving a chance to talk to someone who knew her, even a little. Hopefully, Beverly would be working this morning.

When she walked in, the now familiar scents and sounds surrounded her, a comfort from the rush of changes that were headed her way more quickly than she could have imagined. She wasn't sure what she thought she'd do when she came to Magnolia Key, but it certainly hadn't been to buy the theater. Or have anything to do with a theater. And yet, here she was with her big plans. Excited about them.

Beverly waved to her and motioned for her

to take a seat. She scanned the room, her gaze settling on the only available two-top. As she sat down, she noticed a lone older woman sitting at the table behind her, engrossed in reading the paper. Then she ran her gaze around the cafe and froze. Gavin. Not two tables away. Their eyes met briefly, and he did that infuriating bob of his head before turning back to his meal.

Just great. Way to dampen her day.

Beverly came over. "Morning. Good to see you again. How's the exploring of the town going?"

"It's been... interesting." She paused, wondering if she should tell Beverly her plan. The last person she'd told about it—Gavin—hadn't been impressed. Though, Darlene was a fan of it.

"Interesting? How so?" Beverly prodded.

She took a deep breath. "I went to the old theater. Actually went inside it yesterday. And... I'm thinking of buying it."

A chair scraped and the woman sitting at the table beside her turned to her. "You don't say."

"Miss Eleanor, this is Tori. She's visiting for a bit," Beverly introduced them.

"And you think the theater is a good

investment for some out-of-town stranger to purchase?" Miss Eleanor glared at her.

"No—I—I mean, yes." Why was everyone in this town skeptical of her intentions?

"It's not for sale. Not to be bought by some stranger and torn down and some fancy stick-out-like-a-sore-thumb building put up in its place." Miss Eleanor shook her head.

She glanced over at Gavin and saw he was listening in. She squared her shoulders, waiting for him to join in and rail against her plans. Instead, he sat there listening.

"No, I didn't mean that. I want to buy it and restore it back to the way it was. Like it was when I used to go to plays there with my grandmother."

"That sounds like a nice plan, doesn't it Miss Eleanor?" Beverly asked, like she was trying to ease the tension.

"And if you bought the place, would you be willing to sign an agreement that says you won't tear it down?"

Tori stared at the woman. "I guess so. Why?"

"Because we don't need more things torn down in this town and modern things put up to replace them."

"I plan to renovate it. I just need to get a contractor to look at it. Make sure it's structurally sound, and the wiring is up to code. Get an estimate of what it would cost to restore it."

"I can give you those numbers," Miss Eleanor said, her hands crossed across her chest.

"You can? But how?" Confusion swept through her.

"Because I recently bought the theater, had someone check it out, and got estimates for restoration."

Beverly's mouth dropped open. "You did? You didn't say anything."

"I don't have to tell the whole town my business, now do I?" Miss Eleanor frowned at Beverly.

"But you have it up for sale again?" Tori asked.

"I do. Because if the right buyer came along, I'd sell it. But this way I could keep the wrong buyer from purchasing it and tearing it down."

"Like the rumor about Cliff? Him buying it and tearing it down?" Beverly shook her head.

"My son doesn't have the sense God gave him. I didn't find out soon enough that he'd bought those lots at the end of the boardwalk or I'd have stopped that too."

"Wait, Cliff, the man who wants to tear down the theater is your son?" Tori looked between Beverly and Miss Eleanor.

"Yes. He is. I don't know where I went wrong in raising that boy."

"I'd be very interested in seeing any paperwork you have on the place. Talking to the contractor you contacted."

"Smart businesswoman. Double-checking things. I like that. Where are you staying? I'll send the paperwork over."

"I'm at Bayside B&B."

"And your name?"

"Tori… Ah, Tori Duran."

The woman looked at her closely for a moment. "Okay, Miss Duran. We'll see if we can strike a deal. If you're serious about reopening the theater."

"Oh, I'm serious." She nodded vigorously.

"We'll meet later this week, then, at the Realtor's office." Miss Eleanor rose, put some money on the table, and turned to Gavin. "I know you heard all that. You'll help, of course. Make sure the renovations are done correctly.

Like you did on the lighthouse restoration, no matter what those idiots said about you."

She swiveled to watch Gavin's face, knowing full well he would tell Miss Eleanor no. He wanted nothing to do with her.

But he just bobbed his head and smiled at the woman. "Yes, ma'am. If that's what you want."

Tori's mouth gaped open. "I don't need his… help." She almost said interference.

Miss Eleanor narrowed her eyes. "I don't know you. But I know Gavin. I know he'll stick to restoring it back to how it was, not change everything up. So, that will be in the sales contract too. Take it or leave it." She turned and strode briskly out the door.

"Well, looks like you two will be working together," Beverly said.

He just shrugged. "Looks like it. Don't worry, I won't let her ruin the theater."

Tori glared at Gavin. "Ruin it? It was my idea to restore it in the first place."

"And I guess it's my job to see you do it correctly." Gavin rose, dropped some bills on the table, and crossed to the door.

She stood there simmering in anger as he disappeared.

"He really is a good guy. He'll be a big help to you."

"I don't want his help."

"Ah, well, you'll soon learn that no one in this town gets away with countering Miss Eleanor's... ah... wishes." Beverly shook her head. "Except that son of hers, Cliff." she said under her breath as she walked away.

CHAPTER 9

The weeks flew by in a blur of appointments and decisions. Tori started a large notebook for her plans, carefully keeping track of everything that needed to be done.

She'd extended her stay at the B&B but really did need to find a place to stay long term. Darlene's place was quaint and cozy, but she craved her own space. She'd have to make time to check out what was available on the island.

Then the day finally came that she'd been waiting for. She sat nervously in the lawyer's office, waiting for Miss Eleanor to come and sign the final papers. Her pulse raced, longing for the papers to be signed and the theater to be hers. She wanted to honor her grandmother's legacy and rekindle those childhood memories.

Miss Eleanor came in, nodded to her, and sat down. First they signed a contract that she'd restore the theater back to how it was and that she agreed to Gavin overseeing it. She tried one more time to assure Miss Eleanor this contract wasn't needed. But Miss Eleanor wasn't having it. Then they signed the sale papers as the lawyer read through page after page. Her fingers trembled slightly as she signed the last one.

The theater was *hers*. Excitement swept through her.

She rose from the table and reached out her hand. "Thank you, Miss Eleanor. I promise I won't let you down."

"I expect you won't." The woman nodded. "Because I'll have Gavin there watching to make sure it's done right."

Tori bristled. "I assure you it will be done right. It will be restored to its previous grandeur."

She hurried out into the sunshine, clenching the key tightly in one hand, her notebook in the other. She headed down the sidewalk and directly over to the theater. Bursting with pride, she opened the front door and stepped inside. With determined steps, she headed into the main theater room. Pride mixed with nostalgia washed over her as she ran her fingers over the worn velvet seats.

"Hey, Grams. I did it," she whispered into the silence.

"You often talk to empty rooms?" Gavin's voice came from the doorway, and she whirled around.

"Do you often sneak up on people?" She glared at him, annoyed that he ruined the moment.

"I just stepped in the door. No sneaking involved," he replied with a trace of amusement.

"My grandmother would love knowing this theater was going to be restored and active again." She eyed him defiantly but was surprised to see a slight softening of his normally grumpy demeanor. "What are you doing here?"

"Thought we could look around the whole place. Come up with a plan."

"I have a plan." She held up her large notebook. "Very detailed."

"Great, then let's go over it. Step by step."

She let out a long sigh, the sound echoing in

the vast space of the theater. "Then will you leave me alone?"

"Probably not," he admitted, his features relaxing into the first genuine smile she'd seen from him.

Gavin felt a tiny bit guilty for interrupting Tori's private moment. Some people might think it was a bit weird that the woman talked to her grandmother. But he thought it was kind of endearing.

He swept his gaze around the theater. "Okay, want to start here in the theater?"

"My plans actually start at the front door. It's sturdy but needs to be scraped and repainted. I want to paint it the same green it used to be. And it needs a new lock." She opened the notebook she'd held up and seemed like she was consulting a list. "The ticket booth outside needs to be repaired. It has broken boards. One of the panes of glass in the window that holds the posters of the shows needs to be replaced. And the word 'Theater' over the door is missing the T." Snapping the notebook shut, she walked away from him, heading to the lobby.

He trotted behind her, impressed with her thoroughness so far. She slowly led him around the theater, pointing out what she'd found. Telling him the estimates to fix things. He followed her around, pleased by her attention to detail. Maybe working with her on the restoration wouldn't be as impossible as it first seemed when Miss Eleanor asked him to help out. And it's not like he'd say no to Miss Eleanor.

As she pored over her notebook, a thought popped into his head. "It sounds like it's going to be pretty pricey to fix this up. You took that into consideration with your financing?"

Her expression was guarded when she turned to him. "Not that my finances are any of your concern, but I paid cash. The repairs are not a problem."

He swallowed his surprise. Cash? Who had that kind of cash lying around? He hadn't meant to pry into her financial matters. He just wanted to be sure she could actually swing paying for the repairs.

"Uh, sorry. I just don't want Miss Eleanor to

be disappointed." In the restoration. In him. Because not many people had stood up for him the last time he'd helped the town with a restoration, but Miss Eleanor had. Probably the only reason anyone still spoke to him around town. They had a way of listening to Miss Eleanor.

Clearing his throat, he gestured for her to continue. "Okay, let's keep going."

Hours later, they had gone through all her notes. Tori sank onto one of the seats in the theater, exhaustion lining her face. He sat down beside her and stretched out his legs. "I think that was a productive afternoon."

She raised an eyebrow but didn't say anything.

"You have a very thorough list," he said, trying to bridge the gap between them.

She eyed him with a measured and determined look. "So, you'll back off and let me do this on my own?"

He met her gaze, just as firm and unwavering. "Not a chance."

Tori's brisk walk back to the B&B did little to curb her irritation. This was getting to be her new routine. Get annoyed by Gavin and then walk back to Darlene's with her emotions swirling. Today's walkthrough had been a mix of helpful and exasperating. Each step she took was punctuated by annoyance at his unwelcome and yet annoyingly helpful advice. But now that he'd seen the plans, couldn't he just step away?

Tori approached the B&B and saw Darlene sitting on a rocker on the porch. A tranquil scene compared to her raging thoughts.

"Care to join me? I have a pot of tea here and extra cups. Just needed a few minutes off my feet. Busy day."

Tori sank into the chair next to Darlene and accepted the cup of tea, grateful for the chance to unwind. "I need to sit for a few minutes too. It was quite the day."

"Did you get all the papers signed?"

"I did. The theater is officially mine." The thrill of ownership seeped through her again. "Then I went over to it and…" She let out a long exhale. "Gavin showed up and wanted to see all my plans. He's just so… annoying. I wish Miss Eleanor hadn't insisted he help with the restoration. But I sure couldn't talk her out of it. I tried."

"Eleanor just wants to preserve the island's charm. She's very protective of keeping things the way they are."

Tori frowned. "You know, you're the first person I've ever heard call Miss Eleanor just Eleanor."

Darlene laughed. "We were childhood friends. Grew up together on the island. I pre-date the whole Miss Eleanor name."

"I just wish she'd let me do it alone. I promised her I wouldn't change it. Just restore it. Hopefully, now that Gavin has seen my plans, he'll stay out of my hair."

Darlene looked doubtful. "Maybe. But if Eleanor asked him to keep an eye on the restoration, I'm sure he'll keep his word."

Tori leaned back in her chair, taking a sip of the tea. "Yeah, you're probably right. He seems like a man of his word. She made some comment about him working on the restoration of the lighthouse?"

Darlene hesitated, a bit of a reserved look crossing her face. "Ah, yes. He was involved…"

"And the restorations turned out fine?"

"The lighthouse is working again now, yes," Darlene said with a strange tone to her voice.

Enough talk about Gavin. She'd had enough of him for one day. She steered the conversation in a new direction. "You seem to be really full with guests at the B&B these days."

"It has been busy."

"I plan on finding my own place soon. I just haven't had time to do much looking around."

"I'll miss having you here, but what kind of place are you looking for?"

"An apartment or something simple. I'll be so busy with the theater I won't have much time for upkeep."

"I heard of an apartment in a nice older building right on the gulf. Used to be a huge house. Now it's divided into two living areas. This is the upper level. Heard about it from Beverly. I can make a call and see if you can go see it if you'd like."

"Thank you, I'd love that." A sense of relief washed over her. If she could take this step and find a place to call her own, maybe she'd start feeling more like she belonged here.

"I'll call first thing in the morning and let you know."

"Thank you, Darlene. You've been so helpful with everything."

"I like to keep my guests happy." Darlene smiled. "And besides, after all this time you've been here, I consider you a friend."

A friend. She had a friend in Magnolia. The thought brought an unexpected sense of warmth. Maybe she would find her place here on the island.

CHAPTER 10

The next morning Tori arrived at the address Darlene had given her. She had an appointment with the landlord at ten. As she walked up the sidewalk to the house, she smiled at the long front porch, freshly painted, with a pair of rocking chairs at one end and a porch swing at the other. It was charmingly picture-perfect. She knocked on the door and was greeted by a smiling man in his sixties, she'd guess.

He reached out and took her hand, shaking it warmly. "You must be Tori. I'm Pete."

She smiled at him. "I am."

"Well, come on up and see the place. Both the upstairs and downstairs renters have a key to the front door. Their unit is through there," he pointed to a door to the left, "and the unit for rent is up these stairs."

She followed him up the stairs, and he opened the door for her. "Go ahead," he said as he stepped back.

She stepped inside and the large room spread out before her. Sunlight spilled across the room, and she could hardly contain her delight. High white ceilings with sturdy beams gave the room an airy feel. The hardwood floors were worn but inviting with multiple colorful rugs scattered about. Large windows stretched across the back of the house, perfectly framing a view of the gulf. An unbidden gasp escaped when she stepped over to take in the view. The immense gulf stretched out before her, the turquoise water topped with foamy-tipped waves. The white sand at the edge of the waves shimmered in the morning sunshine, beckoning anyone to come walk on it. She turned to Pete. "This is an amazing view."

He grinned. "Yep, sure is. And wait 'til you see the sunsets from here. They're spectacular."

He showed her the kitchen where more sunlight spilled in on the gleaming cream-colored counters. Warm maple cabinets and shiny stainless appliances greeted her as if asking for someone to come in and cook.

"It was all updated last year," Pete added. "And I'll show you the bedroom."

He continued the tour. "That small bedroom has been used as an office, mostly. Not much in it. You could use it for whatever you like."

They continued down the hall and stepped through the paneled door that was ajar and into the main bedroom. A comfortable queen bed stood on the far side, and the walls were painted a light sea foam green. An overstuffed chair sat by the window with a reading lamp and a small table. The room was cozy and inviting, with lots of closet space.

"Comes furnished. The kitchen is pretty well equipped too. Unless you're some kind of master chef and need fancy equipment."

She turned to him and smiled. "Not much of a cook, I'm afraid. Though that kitchen makes me want to learn."

She swept her gaze around the room one more time before following him out to the main room. "This is just… perfect. Just perfect." She couldn't chase the word home out of her thoughts.

"You need some time to decide?" Pete asked.

"I have decided. I want it. I love it."

"Perfect. It's yours. I have a copy of the lease on the buffet." He walked over and retrieved it.

"Don't you need to run credit checks or something?"

"Nah, if Miss Eleanor was fine doing business with you, then so am I."

She looked at him, slightly surprised he knew all that. But then, it was a small town. And everyone seemed to know each other's business.

They signed the lease, she wrote him a check, and he handed her the key. "All ready whenever you are."

She clutched the key in her hand, happy to have this place of her own.

"If you need anything, just call. My number is on the fridge."

"Thanks, Pete."

He headed down the stairs, whistling as he left. She turned around and flung her arms wide. "I love this place," she said into the empty room.

She could just picture her grandmother's desk in the small bedroom. And she was slightly addicted to her fancy coffee machine. She'd make up a list of things for her assistant to have delivered here. She had a lovely quilt with yellow flowers on it that her grandmother had made. It would look lovely in the bedroom. It had been packed away for years because it didn't fit with her modern apartment in New York. But it would be perfect here. A few of her things would make the place feel like hers.

She glanced at her watch, debating heading to Darlene's to get her things or going to the theater. She did have calls and more decisions to make.

Duty won, and she turned to leave. "But I'll be back," she promised as she walked down the stairs. Peace settled over her, and for the first time in a long time, she felt like she was right where she was meant to be. And had a purpose for her life again.

CHAPTER 11

Annoyance nagged at Gavin all morning. He'd gone by the theater first thing this morning only to find it was locked up tight. A mid-morning trip yielded the same result. Still no sign of Tori.

Was she not serious about this whole project? She just bought it and now felt no urgency to get started on the restorations? He'd made a long list of notes he wanted to go over with her. If she ever showed up…

A lull at The Bike Shop mid-day afforded him another chance to run over to the theater. He called out to Jonny, "Hey, I'm going out for a bit. You got things here?"

"Sure thing. I got this," Jonny called back.

Gavin wiped the grease from his hands.

He'd been working on a bike all morning. Well, at least all morning between trips to the theater. He headed outside, grabbed a bike, and rode over to the theater, fully expecting to see it locked up tight again.

The front door stood ajar. So, she'd finally decided to show up. He strode into the lobby, its neglected, dim interior a marked contrast to the brightness outside. As his eyes adjusted, he spotted her standing at the far side. He didn't even try to temper his annoyance. "I came by first thing this morning. You weren't here. I thought you were serious about getting going on this project." He stopped in his tracks when he got closer and saw her with her hair tied back and lugging a bucket and a squeegee. The window in front of her sparkled.

"I don't run on your schedule," she shot back, planting her hands on her hips.

He stared at the window, then the bucket, then back up to Tori's face. A bit of grime adorned her cheek. She reached up and brushed back a lock of hair while he stared at her. The last thing he ever thought he'd see was Tori in here cleaning. It was a side of her he hadn't anticipated —hands-on and unafraid of getting dirty.

"I just thought you'd be jumping on the project first thing." He still couldn't drag his eyes away from her. She looked incredibly adorable with her hair a mess and the smudge on her face. He had to resist the urge to wipe away the dirt.

"I had something I needed to do."

"More important than this?" He knew he shouldn't have said it the moment the words were out.

"Gavin, I don't report to you. And yes, it was something I had to do. Not that it's any of your business. You can watch over the restoration like Miss Eleanor asked, but you can't watch over me. Get it?" She fired the words at him, her eyes flashing.

He held up both hands in a gesture of surrender. "You're right. I'm sorry."

"Did you need something?" She looked down at the bucket. "I have work to do."

"I... uh... well, I made a list of things I thought of last night after talking to you yesterday."

"I'm fine with my list, just like it is."

"But—"

"No, seriously. Unless you think I'm doing

something Miss Eleanor won't like with the restoration, then just butt out. I've got this."

And he was certain that she did have this. But he did have some ideas about how she could save money. But obviously, now was not the time. Her annoyance with him was evident in the set of her shoulders and the way she clenched her jaw.

"How about I help you clean the windows?"

Her mouth dropped open. "Why would you do that?"

"Because if we both work on it, we'll get them cleaned up faster."

"You don't have to do that."

"But I want to. Let me help."

She stared at him for a moment. "There are more buckets and squeegees in the storeroom."

He nodded and walked away, returning soon with his own supplies. They worked side by side —silently—until every window in the lobby was crystal clear. The lobby slowly transformed as sunlight filtered in through the now gleaming windows. She set down her bucket and swept her gaze around the lobby. "That looks better."

"It does." He agreed. "Now what?"

"Well, everything needs a good cleaning, but the windows were bugging me the most, so

I started there. I'll need to get someone with a large ladder or platform to clean the chandelier. I'm going to vacuum every single seat in the theater too. It's been sitting here collecting dust for so long." She shoved back her hair again and swiped at her face, but only managed to add another streak of dirt to her fair skin.

"You could hire this out," he suggested.

"I will for things I can't do myself. But I can do a lot of it myself. I do have the contractor coming tomorrow with his workers. Electrician, plumber, and some carpenters. I've hired someone to come out and steam clean the stage curtain."

"Then let me help you. I want to help you. I enjoy watching old buildings come back to life."

"Like the lighthouse?"

He flinched slightly. He still could barely stand to even think about that project. He just bobbed his head in answer.

She set her squeegee in the bucket and looked at him for a long minute. "Okay, I'll accept your help under one condition."

"What's that?"

"You don't tell me how to do things."

He could do that, couldn't he? Probably.

Maybe. But he nodded his head in agreement. "Sure thing, boss." He winked at her.

She just rolled her eyes. "Anyway, I'm calling it quits for today. I have to pack up my things. I found an apartment and I'm going to move in tonight. I've already called Darlene and told her I'm checking out of the B&B. And I want to go get some groceries for the place."

"You're going to do all that after doing all this? Aren't you tired?"

"A bit. But I'm excited about moving into my own place."

"I could help you." The words came out unexpectedly.

She shook her head. "Thanks, but I've got it. I only have a few suitcases right now. I'm going to send for some of my things now that I have a place."

"So, I'll see you here tomorrow?"

"I'll be here early. I'm meeting the contractor at seven. But you don't have to be here then. I've got it."

He nodded. But he had every intention of being here at seven a.m. sharp. And he was going to find a way to talk to her about a few of the suggestions he'd thought of. But it would be better to do at a time when he hadn't annoyed her quite so much. He grinned to himself. If that ever happened.

Tori swung by the market and got some groceries and supplies for her new apartment. Then she went to Darlene's and packed up her things. She carted her suitcases down the stairs and Darlene greeted her in the foyer, her eyes holding a warmth that expressed more than just a casual host-guest relationship.

"I'm going to miss having you here." Darlene hugged her.

"I'll miss you too." She hugged her back, lingering momentarily, sad to be leaving her newfound friend.

"You come over any time to visit. We'll grab tea and sit on the porch," Darlene insisted as she grabbed one of the suitcases.

"I will, I promise."

They carried the suitcases to her car and loaded them into the back seat.

Tori climbed into the car and waved as she pulled away. It was a quick drive over to her apartment, and the sound of the crushed shell drive welcomed her as she parked in her space.

She tugged a suitcase from the back seat and headed inside. Once upstairs, she set the suitcase down, smiling at the late afternoon sun spilling into the room with a warm, inviting embrace. Yes, this could definitely feel like home.

By the last trip up the stairs, she was out of breath. She was beginning to see the allure of a ground-floor apartment. But as she closed her door and looked out at the beginning of a sunset sprawling before her, she knew there was nowhere she'd rather be. And hopefully, she wouldn't have to make so many trips up and down those stairs again anytime soon.

She unpacked her suitcases and hung up her clothes, then moved on to putting her toiletries in the spacious bathroom. Then she moved on to the kitchen, unloading the groceries and supplies. She sank onto a chair at the wooden table, so very tired, and looked around the place with a mixture of fatigue and satisfaction. This was all hers.

Hunger nagged at her, but she had little motivation to cook. But she had to eat something. She shoved off the chair and grabbed a pack of microwave popcorn. That would do. She poured herself a glass of wine while her dinner cheerily popped in the microwave. Simple feast in hand, she nestled into a chair by the window, propping up her feet and enjoying the solitude.

She took a sip of her wine, and Gavin popped into her mind. He'd annoyed her so much when he showed up today, like he ruled her schedule. But then he surprised her by helping with the windows. Teetering back to annoyance, she remembered he'd initially come to give her a list of suggestions. His interference was a constant aggravation. She could only hope that after he saw she was doing a good job, he'd back off.

Leaning back in the chair, she pushed all thoughts of Gavin, of any aggravation, far from her mind. As she ate her popcorn, a dark orange slash of color conveyed the end of the sunset. She sat there watching the sky darken and the stars come out, enjoying the quiet. Enjoying the view. Just... enjoying this life she was creating here on Magnolia Key.

CHAPTER 12

Tori got up early the next morning and grabbed a cup of coffee while she got ready, her new routine beginning to feel familiar. As she glanced in the mirror, she realized she was getting used to her new look, too.

Her normally pale skin had tanned slightly from being outside so often walking around town. Her hair that she used to spend so much time using expensive products on and curling—*just right*—hung loosely at shoulder length. She was beginning to feel less anxious that someone would recognize her. Victoria Duran was slowly fading away.

So much had changed in her life in the last few months. She'd first felt lost and alone when her world had been upended, but now she was beginning to feel like this was where she was meant to be. And she could feel fulfilled and happy with this life. If she'd let herself…

She tidied the bathroom, set the coffee mug in the kitchen, and headed out to the theater. Walking, of course. She wished she had time to go to Beverly's and chat with her, but she wanted to make sure she was at the theater before Gavin showed up.

She hurried down the sidewalk, then laughed at herself as she slowed down to enjoy the walk. The sleepy town was waking up. People smiled at her when they passed instead of ducking their heads to avoid eye contact, which happened so often in New York. Everyone busy with their own thoughts, own problems, and rushing past. The warm sun slipped from behind a fluffy white cloud, and sunlight danced through the palm branches. The day was shaping up to be a wonderful one. Full of promise.

She walked up to the front door, unlocked it, and stepped inside, once again overwhelmed with the responsibility of the job she'd taken on. And just as sure that she'd made the right decision. The lobby was already more inviting now that the windows were cleaned of years of grime. She went over to the concession counter where she'd set her notebook.

"I see you're here early today."

Startled, she dropped her pen and turned around at the sound of Gavin's voice, trying to mask her surprise. "Ah... good morning." She didn't know if he meant it as a compliment or still a chastisement over her late arrival yesterday. Luckily, she didn't have to muse on it long because the contractor she'd hired stepped inside and joined them.

"Morning, Miss Duran."

"Please, call me Tori." The less the name Duran was thrown around, the better. "Let's get started."

Soon more workers arrived, and the sounds of saws and hammers rang through the building. Gavin stood beside her, looking over her shoulder, annoying her, as she turned the pages of her notebook, making sure she hadn't forgotten anything.

"I know you don't like to be told what to do... but I do have something I thought I should mention."

"Of course you do. So much for not interfering and telling me what to do."

"I just thought we needed to check out the

machines at the concession stand. I don't think that was on your list."

Annoyingly, it wasn't. She grabbed her notebook. She'd check out the popcorn machine and soda dispensers. The candy counter was still in good shape, though.

"And I had another thought..." He stood back, eyeing her, waiting.

She let out a sigh. "Go ahead."

"Some theaters have gone to serving wine. If we got a license, then people who rented the space for events would have the opportunity to serve wine if they wanted."

She grudgingly admitted he had a good idea. She scribbled more notes, only slightly less annoyed at him for his ideas. They were good ones.

"I'm going to go grab a hammer and work on the ticket counter outside. I'm pretty handy with stuff like that." He turned and walked out the door. She hoped his skills were as good as he claimed.

She couldn't believe that she walked right past this concession stand at the side of the lobby every time she'd been here but hadn't thought to check out the machines. She thought she'd been so thorough.

Maybe it wasn't so bad to have a second set of eyes on her plans. And of course, Gavin would speak up if he thought she was missing anything. She laughed. She was almost getting used to his interference. Almost.

The weeks passed in a blur. Each day was a blend of working at the theater and coming home to crash in her apartment. Gavin became a constant figure at the theater, showing up almost every day for some amount of time. She questioned him, asking if he didn't need to be at his bike shop, but he said he had it covered. She got the impression he was actually enjoying working on the theater. She'd grown accustomed to his presence... mostly.

They'd begun talking a lot as they worked side by side. He was an interesting guy, she had to admit. And boy, did he have opinions about everything. Some of them were even right.

She grinned as she worked on cleaning out one of the dressing rooms. A musty smell permeated the room. She went over and struggled to open a window, managing to slide it up enough to let in some fresh air.

Old play pamphlets were heaped on a table. Costumes were scattered around in piles. She'd leave the programs for now, but the costumes had to be dealt with. She fingered the fabric of a long ballgown, then the smooth silk of a 1920s flapper dress, wondering what roles had been played in these costumes.

She made trip after trip, hauling them over to the costume area. Hanging them up. Trying to get some sort of order to all of them. When those were all finally sorted out, she returned to the dressing room and crossed over to the closet on the far side, hoping there weren't yet more costumes inside. She tugged on the door, but it didn't budge.

"Want some help?"

She whirled around, her heart skipping a beat, startled by Gavin's voice. He had a way of surprising her. "I… uh… the door is stuck."

"Let me give it a try."

He walked over and jiggled the handle, but had no more luck than she did. She stood back, patiently watching as he wrestled with the door. "It's stuck." He finally gave up in defeat.

"That's what I said." Amusement tugged the corners of her mouth.

"Let me get some tools." He came back and

set to work on the door while she sorted through the programs. She set aside some that were in good shape to frame and put up in the lobby.

"There, got it," he announced triumphantly with a flourish of his arm.

The closet door stood wide open. She crossed over and peeked inside, struggling to see into the depths. "I thought it was just a tiny closet. It's larger than I thought."

Gavin tapped on the flashlight on his phone and raised it high. "It is rather large. Here's a light switch." He clicked it on, but nothing happened. "Let me go get a ladder and a lightbulb. I'll be back."

She turned back to her project, sorting through the programs while Gavin worked on the light. Soon light spilled out from the closet and she went over to look at it again.

"Oh, wow. Look at this. It must have been a private dressing room." A fancy dressing table surrounded by lights sat on one end. A neon star adorned the wall across from it. A single clothes rack was tucked into the corner and an old, faded sofa sat under the star.

"Looks like it."

She closed her eyes against the wave of memories flooding back. Her own dressing room with her name on the door. The lights surrounding her reflection in the mirror as the hairstylist would do her hair each night—hair without even one strand of gray in it— and the makeup artist applying her stage makeup.

"You okay?" Gavin looked at her closely.

"What?" She turned to him slowly. "Yes, I'm… fine."

"You kind of look like you've seen a ghost. You think this theater has one?" He teased her.

"I doubt it." She pulled herself together and walked over to the dressing table. She slowly pulled open the drawers to look inside. Old makeup. Some brushes and combs. A fancy hair clip. She tugged on the bottom drawer, but it was stuck. Why was everything sticking on her today?

"Let me look at it," Gavin said, walking over and jiggling the drawer before dropping down to the floor and peeking underneath it. "Something's caught. There, try it again."

She pulled on the drawer and it slid open. "All that work for an empty drawer."

He crawled out from under the dressing table and looked at the drawer. "Can't be. Something made it stick." He felt around in the drawer, then finally pulled it out all the way and sat it on the table, frowning. He held it up, scrutinized it, and then pushed on the back section. A board popped open.

They leaned over the drawer. "Oh, a pendant." She reached out and picked it up, tracing her finger over it. It's lovely, isn't it? I wonder if it was a prop in some show."

"Why would someone hide a prop? That doesn't make much sense, does it?"

"No, I guess not." She held it up to the light, examining it closely. "Look, it has a magnolia on it. And I think these are diamonds and emeralds, aren't they? Or I guess they could be crystals."

"You should have it looked at."

She wrapped her fingers around it, feeling it warm to her touch. "I wonder what the story is behind this?"

"I'm sure I don't know. But Beverly or Miss Eleanor might. They pretty much know everything there is to know about the island."

She slipped it in her pocket, making a mental note to talk to both of them about it.

"I've got to go," he said as he packed up his tools.

"So soon?" she asked, both surprised and

annoyed at her disappointment that he was leaving already.

"Got to go back to the shop. Have some repairs to finish up."

She nodded. "Okay. See you tomorrow."

"Yep. Tomorrow." He strode out of the room and she stood there, the emptiness of the room echoing around her.

She closed her eyes against the memories. The thrill of getting ready for a performance. The jittery nerves of opening nights. The hours spent memorizing lines. The costume fittings. All of it.

But that was no longer her life, she reminded herself. This was. Bringing Magnolia Key Theater back to life.

Now that the renovations were moving along, it was time to look into getting a traveling troupe to perform for their grand opening. Then she had plans to try to do some local theater. See if any residents wanted to perform. And she'd see if she could get more actors from the mainland. Fill the seats like they used to be. Bring life back into this magnificent theater. It's what it deserved. To be alive and full of people.

She walked over and flipped off the lights,

leaving the star's dressing room and the memories behind her.

CHAPTER 13

Beverly wiped down the counter at Coastal Coffee the next morning, the familiar routine comforting and grounding. The cafe hummed with the bustle of the morning regulars. Nash had come and gone. Miss Eleanor was sitting at her usual table, immersed in the paper.

Maxine walked up to the counter. "At least I remembered to bring Miss Eleanor's cream in her own special pitcher." She grinned. "So I don't get *that look* from her."

"You are catching on." Beverly laughed. The presence of her best friend brought an added warmth to Coastal Coffee. She loved having her best friend working with her. Maxine seemed to have settled in nicely to island life. It didn't hurt that she was dating Dale now. She'd seen them out to dinner at Sharky's and knew they'd had a beach picnic dinner just last week. It was heartwarming to see her friend was so happy here.

She reached out and touched Maxine's hand. "You know. I'm really glad you returned to Magnolia Key. Glad you're working here. Just... happy to have my best friend back."

Maxine smiled and squeezed her hand. "I'm happy too. Best decision I've made in a really long time."

The door opened, bringing in a rush of the fresh morning air. She waved as Tori headed their direction. "Morning, Tori. Haven't seen you much since you started on those theater renovations."

Tori slid onto a barstool. "I know. I've been so busy. But I wanted to come in today and show you something."

Beverly put down her towel. "Oh? What do you want to show me?"

"This." Tori took a gold pendant out of her pocket and set it on the counter. "I found it hidden in a drawer in a dressing room at the theater."

Beverly picked it up, eyeing it carefully, her

fingers tracing its edges. "It's very pretty. Looks kind of old, doesn't it? And there's a magnolia on it. And maybe diamonds and emeralds?"

Maxine leaned in for a closer look. "Sure look like diamonds to me."

"Unless it was just a prop. Then they might be crystals. But why would someone hide a prop?" Tori's forehead wrinkled. "But I thought you might have some idea of whose it is?"

"We could ask Miss Eleanor if she's seen it before," Beverly suggested.

Miss Eleanor eyed them suspiciously as they approached. "Yes?" Annoyance was etched into the lines on her face at the interruption.

"Tori found this pendant at the theater. Hidden in a drawer. Do you recognize it?" Beverly held it out to Miss Eleanor.

She took one look at it and her eyes narrowed as she thrust it back to Beverly. "No clue. Now, can I eat my meal in peace?"

"Sure. Sorry to bother you," Beverly quickly appeased her. "Can I bring you more coffee?"

"Yes." Miss Eleanor nodded and turned back to the newspaper she was reading.

They went back to the counter and Tori sat back down as Beverly went behind the counter and Maxine went to get more coffee for Miss Eleanor.

"Did you see her? I think she recognized it." Tori frowned, clearly puzzled. "But why wouldn't she tell us where she'd seen it?"

"We've had a lot of that from her," Beverly said in a low voice so Miss Eleanor wouldn't hear them. "I found an old rolled-up canvas hidden in the bookcase in my office. And Maxine found a hidden letter in a purse she picked up at Dale's Second Finds. But the letter didn't make any sense, really. And it was just signed V. We showed both to Miss Eleanor and I swear she knows something about them. But she just acts like she has no clue. Not sure why." She shrugged.

"That's kind of strange."

Maxine came back from refilling Miss Eleanor's coffee. "I think she's seen that pendant before."

"We were just both saying that." Beverly nodded. "Hey, speaking of Dale…"

As Dale walked up to them, Maxine's eyes lit up, and a smile brightened her face. "Hi," she said softly to Dale.

Dale smiled back at her, and for a moment, it was just the two of them. Beverly was certain no one else in the cafe existed for them. She smiled to herself, pleased with how things were progressing for Maxine and Dale. She gave them their moment, then cleared her throat. "Dale, have you met Tori yet?"

"No, I haven't." He pulled his gaze from Maxine and smiled at Tori. "But I've seen her around town. Heard you're the one restoring the theater. Very happy to see that."

"Nice to meet you," Tori said.

Dale turned to Maxine. "I just wanted to make sure we're on for our date tonight."

"We're on. Six o'clock?" Maxine blushed just the tiniest bit, and Beverly smothered a smile.

Beverly switched her attention to Dale. "Hey, look at this." She held out the pendant and turned to explain to Tori, "He's kind of our history buff around here."

He took it and looked at it carefully. "It looks old. At least a hundred years, I'd estimate. Maybe more. And if I'm not mistaken, those are real diamonds and emeralds. That must be worth a pretty penny."

"I found it hidden in a drawer at the theater."

"Interesting." Dale looked at it again. "Let

me take some photos of it, and I'll do some research. See if I can find out anything. I would think someone would remember a pendant this remarkable. I'll let you know if I discover anything."

"Thank you. I'd appreciate it." Tori nodded.

Dale took a series of photos and handed the pendant back to Tori. "Well, I better run now. Just wanted to check in." He reached out and squeezed Maxine's hand. "See you tonight."

Dale left and Tori ordered her breakfast. "Maxine, why don't you sit? Things are slowing down now. Let's join Tori for coffee."

When Tori's order was up, Beverly brought it to her. Then she stood behind the counter making napkin rolls and chatting with her and Maxine. "So, Tori, how are the renovations going?"

"They are going really well. Nothing big that was missed on my plans. Well, except for the new popcorn machine and the soda dispensers. Those needed to be replaced. Gavin noticed I didn't have them listed in my plans."

"That Gavin is a stickler for details. When the lighthouse was being restored…" Beverly paused. "Well, let's just say he wanted things done a certain way. He has… opinions."

"I'll say he does. Lots of them." Tori laughed with a twinge of amusement in her tone. "And the annoying thing? His suggestions usually have at least the hint of a good idea in them."

"I haven't seen him around much since I've been back," Maxine added.

"He's kind of a loner these days. Ever since the whole lighthouse restoration." Beverly wasn't sure how much more to say.

"Why is that?" Tori prodded.

"Well… things got a little bit difficult for him during that project. The town got a bit, ah… critical. He pulled back. Been pretty much a loner since then."

"That's too bad. I remember him as an outgoing kid when we were growing up," Maxine said.

"He was. Then he moved away for years. Suddenly, he was back in town. Opened The Bike Shop. He was more reserved than I remember him as a kid." Beverly shrugged. "But who knows? We don't really ever know what's happened in someone's personal life, do we?"

Tori stared at her coffee mug, her expression

thoughtful. "No, we don't, do we?" she said softly.

Beverly got the feeling Tori was talking more about herself than Gavin.

More customers came in and she excused herself, her mind still full of questions about the pendant and wondering what secrets Tori might be hiding. But of course, it was none of her business.

CHAPTER 14

L ate the next afternoon, after spending most of the day cleaning, Tori stood at the table in the dressing room, finishing up sorting through the old programs. She had a box of ones she wanted to keep, a few she wanted to frame, and some she planned to just recycle. She couldn't think of a good reason to keep hundreds of extra old programs.

As she sorted through the last stack, she noticed they were all very old, the paper wrinkled and faded. She opened one and smiled. They'd done a musical adaptation of *Show Boat*. She loved the songs in the musical. A Vera Whitmore had played the part of Magnolia Hawks, the riverboat captain's daughter. She carefully put a few copies of the program aside in the frame pile.

She turned at the sound of a knock. Gavin stood in the doorway with a tool belt slung low on his hips, a smile teasing at his lips. "You look immersed in those programs."

"And you managed to enter the room without startling me," she shot back, self-consciously wiping the dust from her hands. It seemed like every project at the theater involved grime or dust, and he was always seeing her at her worst.

"I finished up the last coat of paint on the outside ticket booth. And I checked and the popcorn machine will be delivered tomorrow."

She pushed back a lock of her hair, one hand on her lower back.

"You look beat," he said, eyeing her with a small frown.

"I am tired. It's been a long day."

"You should quit. Rest. Get something to eat."

"You're probably right. But I have to go to the market and get groceries. I noticed this morning that I'm out of almost everything."

"Let's go grab something to eat at Sharky's," he offered up so nonchalantly.

She looked at him in surprise. "Us?"

"I mean, I'm hungry. You're hungry. We both like Sharky's."

As tiredness swept over her, she still hesitated. But she didn't know if she had the energy to shop and cook. "Okay, yes. That's a good idea."

His offer triggered distant memories of late post-show meals with her castmates, their conversations animated from the adrenaline of their performances. But this acceptance was more a response to her exhaustion. The lesser of two evils, not that she'd tell him that.

"Let me just grab this box of recycling to put in our stack in the lobby."

"Oh, I already hauled off the recycling earlier this afternoon. But we can start another stack. And I mentioned to the workers to make sure they recycle all that they can."

His diligence to detail brought back a fleeting memory of the favorite stagehand who always checked to make sure her props were in place and everything was exactly right for her performance. She should have thanked him more often.

"Thank you for doing all that," she said with more gratitude than the situation warranted, trying to make up for her past omissions and hoping Gavin would quit stirring up memories better forgotten.

He reached over and picked up the box. "Coming?"

She followed him through the theater, turning off lights as they went. He set the box down in the corner of the lobby, and she saw there was now a sign on the wall that said recycling here.

"Walking okay? Or are you too tired?" He eyed her as if he expected her to admit how tired she actually was.

"No, walking is fine." They stepped out into the evening light and she locked the door. The fresh air revived her as they headed to the boardwalk. She hurried a bit to keep up with his long strides, and he seemed to notice and slowed his pace.

"Lucky to have this breeze tonight. Chasing away the humidity."

"It is nice."

"Supposed to be much warmer tomorrow, though."

So they were reduced to talking about the weather? Well, she guessed that was better than him spouting off his opinions.

They headed into Sharky's and it took a minute for her eyes to adjust to the dimness of the interior. He waved to Sharky, who motioned for them to take a seat. Though this wasn't the original Sharky. Not the older man who ran it when she was young and came with her grandmother. It was Sharky's nephew or someone like that. But everyone still called him Sharky.

"Let's grab a table." He strode across the room, weaving between the tables, and sat at a booth in the corner.

She slid into the seat across from him. The server came, and they both ordered the fried grouper and a beer. They got their drinks, and she settled back into her seat, glad to be off her feet.

"So, you're a fan of their grouper too?" he asked.

"I am. I had it so many times when I came here with Grams."

"So you two were close?"

"We were. I… I miss her."

"You have any other family?"

"Just a brother and a niece."

"No ex-husband or kids?"

"No… no husband, ex or otherwise. You?"

"It's just me now. I was an only child and my parents are gone."

No family at all? That must be hard. And she felt strangely bonded to him with his lack of children too. So many people questioned her choices. But when she was younger, of the childbearing age, her career had taken off. She'd dated some back then, but no one really seriously. Then she'd had a string of fairly permanent boyfriends that lasted from a few years to maybe five. But something always eventually went wrong.

"Penny for your thoughts." He smiled at her.

"Oh, I was just thinking about life choices."

He nodded as if he understood. "We make them not always knowing their far-reaching effects, don't we?"

"We do."

"So, you don't talk much about your past life. What did you do before you came to the island?"

And there it was. The question she'd been dreading. It was like a spotlight's glare just focused on her. "I—"

Their meals were delivered just then, giving her an excuse to stay quiet.

But after the server left, Gavin wouldn't let it go. "You were saying?"

"I worked in the theater district." That was close enough for the truth, wasn't it?"

"Really? No wonder you were interested in buying the theater. What did you do?"

"I... um... worked on productions."

"Oh, like backstage stuff? That sounds interesting."

She didn't bother to correct him. She changed the subject. "And what did you do before you came back to Magnolia?"

He gave a wry laugh. "I was the head of community outreach for a large nonprofit in Los Angeles. In charge of all the fundraising."

"So going out and actually talking to people to get them to donate?" She tried to hide her surprise.

"Yeah, stuff like that." He took a bite of his sandwich, ignoring her look.

"So is that why you helped with the lighthouse restoration? To raise money for it?"

"I... uh... kind of."

She wasn't sure what happened with Gavin and the lighthouse restoration, but she got the feeling she shouldn't press it anymore.

She changed the subject again. "So, has Miss Eleanor been asking you about the theater restoration and how's it going?"

"No, I think she trusts me."

She set her fork down. "But admit it, I'm doing a good job of it, aren't I? It's turning out nicely. And we're getting close to finishing. Then I just need to make sure I have the opening play lined up... and I almost do. We'll have a grand opening. Then we'll open it up for other events."

"It will be nice to have another larger venue for town events. We've mostly been using the large gazebo in the city park for events since the theater closed."

"Why did it close?"

"I think repairs and upkeep got too expensive. The owner died, and his kids inherited it and had no interest in putting money into it."

"And you didn't want to try to fundraise money from the town to open it?"

He looked at her, his eyes hard and shuttered. "Nope. Not a chance. Not after the lighthouse."

How many times was she going to have to change the subject tonight? Instead, she dug into her dinner as the silence grew between them.

They finished their meals with just a bit of small talk between them. He started to pay for both of them, but she insisted on paying her half.

When they stepped outside, the night sky greeted them, now speckled with stars and a bright moon hovering over the water, casting silvery light over the tops of the waves. She turned to him. "Thanks for inviting me to come along. It was nice having company for a meal."

He nodded. "I'll walk you home."

"You don't have to."

"And yet, I do. That's how I was raised."

They fell into step again, and this time, he kept his stride shorter and slower as they walked down the boardwalk. They cut across to her apartment and walked up the steps of the porch.

"Well, good night, then. I guess I'll see you tomorrow."

"Night." He stepped back and started to turn, then stopped. "Hey, Tori. Thanks for joining me." And with that, he trotted down the stairs and off down the sidewalk.

She slowly climbed the stairs to her

apartment and unlocked the door. As she stepped inside, the now familiar apartment welcomed her.

It had been an… interesting… night. Gavin was an enigma. Sometimes grumpy, sometimes helpful, sometimes secretive.

But then, she had secrets of her own, didn't she?

Gavin slowly walked back to his home. He passed a few other people, some who said hello, some who barely nodded. That had been his lot in this town since the whole lighthouse episode.

But that hadn't really been his fault. His words had been twisted. The media could say whatever they wanted and some people blindly believed it.

He couldn't change that. At least Miss Eleanor had stood up for him. And he appreciated that. He still remembered the day she strode into his shop.

"Gavin, those people are idiots. Don't pay any attention to them."

He'd looked up in surprise.

"Those people have a way of twisting things

around. Try to ignore it all. I believe you." Then she'd turned and walked out the door. Slowly, some of the people in the town had come around. But some of them? They still distrusted him.

But now, he always avoided the media. If he heard the paper was covering something, he wouldn't show up. He knew all too well that some people in the media would just make things up to sell their news. It had happened to him twice now, and he'd learned his lesson the hard way.

He took a deep breath and shoved his thoughts away. He continued his leisurely pace, enjoying the warm evening breeze and the scent of the salty air.

His thoughts slipped back to dinner with Tori. He felt like she was holding back something about herself. But then, he was reserved too, so how could he blame her?

He had come to respect her work ethic. Things were really coming along nicely. And she was *almost* as detail-oriented as he was. At least she didn't call him picky, like most people. She understood him.

He got to his house and went inside, flipping on the lamp near the door. The low light barely illuminated the room, but he was okay with that. He crossed to the fridge, pulled out a beer, then headed out to the deck. He sank onto a chair and took a swallow of the cold liquid.

Thoughts of Tori flickered through his mind. The day she'd painted the dressing room and flecks of cream-colored paint had speckled her cheeks. The way her eyes flashed when he said something that annoyed her.

And he had to admit, occasionally, he'd say something just to see that look of hers. His lips curved into an unbidden smile.

These weeks working at the theater had brought back a sense of purpose to his life. Not that he didn't enjoy owning his bike shop. He did. But it seemed like a bigger purpose to restore the theater. Open it up again. Give something back to the town.

But then, that had been his reasoning on the lighthouse restorations too, and he saw how that went for him. His stomach knotted with a familiar mix of frustration and regret.

He took another swig of the beer and looked up at the sky, his eyes tracing the constellations. The vastness of the universe sprawled out before him.

Then, just like that, she was back in his

thoughts. Her smile. The way she had a habit of pushing back that one always-wayward lock of hair.

He wasn't sure what was coming over him. Or if he liked it. But the woman was getting under his skin.

CHAPTER 15

Gavin arrived at the theater mid-morning the next day after opening The Bike Shop and turning it over to Jonny to run for a few hours. As he walked up the steps he smiled at the freshly painted doors and repaired marquee over the entrance. Things were really shaping up. He stepped inside to the smell of fresh paint and newly scrubbed floors. The lights were on, so he knew Tori must be here working somewhere. The subcontractor had finished his work, so it was just the last-minute things Tori was finishing up. And he was here to help with that. But after his mixed feelings last night, he figured it would be best if he just got to work. He headed over to the concession stand to hook up the new soda dispenser.

Despite being a handy person, the setup fought him at every turn. Cords and tubes tumbled in a tangled mess. The connections defied his efforts as frustration spread through him. He placed his hands on the counter, annoyed.

A scream shattered the silence of the lobby. The wrench slipped through his hands and clattered to the floor as he sped across the lobby, his footsteps ringing through the empty room. He raced into the main theater, his heart pounding.

"Tori?" he called out, his word swallowed in the vastness of the hall.

He heard a slight moan down by the stage and ran down the aisle, his heart pounding as he saw her lying on the floor. He raced over and knelt beside her. "Tori? Are you hurt?"

"No." She moved slightly and grimaced. "At least I don't think so."

He ran his gaze over her, looking for blood, trying to remain calm.

"I just got the wind knocked out of me. Help me sit up," Tori commanded.

"Absolutely not. Just stay where you are. What happened?"

"I... fell off the edge of the stage. I was

kneeling at the edge and then I turned to shove that box out of the way and I… I slipped off."

"That's quite a fall." He peered up at the stage, judging the distance of her fall. Five or six feet.

She started to sit up. "Ouch."

"What? What hurts?"

"You mean besides my pride? My ankle."

He gently ran his hands over her ankle. "We should go get this x-rayed."

"No, look. I can move it. I just sprained it or something. I'll be fine." She slowly moved her foot this way and that, but he could see a hint of pain flicker in her eyes.

"I think you should get it looked at." He was holding firm to his opinion.

"Gavin, I heard you. But I'm fine."

He looked at her doubtfully. Why wouldn't she just listen? She really should get checked out.

"So, are you going to help me up or do I have to just sit here for the rest of the day?"

Against his better judgment, he gently placed his hands under her arms and helped her to stand, holding her while she caught her balance. "Are you sure you're okay?"

"I'm sure."

"Let's at least put some ice on it. I'll take you back to your office, and then go run and get some ice."

She nodded. "That's probably a good idea. Keep the swelling down."

"Lean on me."

She leaned against him, and he wound his arm around her waist, supporting her, protecting her. If only he'd been here to prevent her fall.

They slowly made their way to her office, his arm still firmly around her. He helped her settle on her chair, suddenly acutely aware she was no longer in his arms.

"There. See? I'm fine." She eyed him defiantly, but her eyes betrayed her bravado. He could tell she was in pain.

"Right." He shook his head. "Stay there until I get back." He headed toward the door and looked back at her. "Please?"

"Okay, okay. I'll still be sitting here when you return."

He walked outside, saw the sign for Coastal Coffee, and figured that was the closest place for ice. He hurried down the sidewalk. As he pushed through the door, he spied Beverly

128

across the room and hurried over to her. "Beverly, I need some ice. Tori took a fall."

"Is she all right?" Beverly's eyes filled with concern.

"I told her she needed to go get checked out, but she refused. Her ankle is starting to swell, so I need ice for it."

"Let me get you a bag of it." Beverly hurried away and returned with a large bag full of ice. "Here. Are you going to stay with her for a while to make sure she's okay? Did she hit her head?"

He frowned. "I don't think so. I should have asked." He chastised himself. "She really should go get looked at."

"Just keep an eye on her. And I'll send lunch over for you two. Tell her just to rest."

"Thanks, Beverly." He hurried out the door, thinking maybe he shouldn't have left Tori alone. Guilt threatened to engulf him as he quickened his pace.

Annoyance crept through Tori. How could she have been so clumsy? It was foolish to be balancing that close to the edge of the stage, especially when she knew better. She'd been performing for years. How many times had she been warned not to get near the edge during her career? And when she was downstage, the edge never worried her. It was like she had an instinctive feeling for where it ended. Though, not today.

She eyed her notebook, sitting across the room on a table. She pushed up from her chair, wincing as she put her weight on her foot. Okay, maybe not such a good idea. She sank back down, thinking she probably should prop up her foot. She pulled out a file drawer and raised her leg, setting her foot on it. That would work for now.

She took a steadying breath. She had to admit, the fall had frightened her. Those split seconds when she knew she was going to fall and could feel the empty air as she struggled to save herself. She had caught herself slightly with her arm, which had helped. She raised her arm and sighed. A nasty bruise was beginning to form under her arm.

She leaned back in her chair. Thank goodness Gavin had been here to help her up. Would she have had to crawl over to one of the seats to pull herself up? He'd looked so concerned for her. But she was okay. Really. She'd just take it easy for a few days. Stay off her foot. But what lousy timing. She still had so much left to do with the grand opening quickly approaching. Dress rehearsals were coming up. The traveling troupe needed at least a few rehearsals to get used to the space. And the lighting crew needed to work with them. And the sound system still had a few kinks that needed to be worked out of it.

Determined, she rose again to go get her notebook. She had to make sure all this got scheduled properly. She could do this. She *had* to do this.

"Don't even think about it." Gavin's voice cut across the room. "What do you think you're doing?" His eyes flashed with aggravation and disbelief.

"Going to get my notebook."

"I'll get it. Sit."

"Don't bark orders at me." Though she had to admit, sitting sounded preferable to walking right now.

He grabbed the notebook, set it on the desk, and motioned to the chair. She sat back down.

He looked down at her makeshift footstool. "Let me at least get something to put on top of that drawer." He returned with a pillow from the prop room and placed it on top of the file drawer. She put her foot up, and he positioned the ice on her ankle.

After she was settled, he looked at her closely. "Hey, did you hit your head?"

"No."

He nodded quickly, and a look of relief swept across his face. He stepped back. "Beverly said she was sending over lunch. And she said to take it easy."

"I won't be running a marathon any time soon. But I do have work to do."

"Give me a list. I'll help. I was working on hooking up the soda dispenser, but that can wait. What do you need done?"

"I have calls to make. I'll be fine now that I have my notebook. You can go back and work on the concession stand."

"I'm not sure I can trust you to stay off your feet." He scowled.

"Gavin, I appreciate your help. But quit hovering. I'm fine. It's just a little bruise or twist." She said the words firmly but wasn't sure if she was trying to convince Gavin or herself.

"Okay, but I'll be back to check on you."

"I'm sure you will." She motioned him to scoot. He walked out of the room, still scowling.

She opened the notebook, took out her phone, and started on her list, ignoring the pain in her ankle.

Gavin came in and ate lunch with her after Beverly's lunch was delivered. She had to practically shove him back out the door of her office when they'd finished.

By late afternoon, she had to admit, the pain was worse. Gavin poked his head in for like the hundredth time. "You doing okay?"

"I…" She sighed. "No, you've got me second-guessing myself. I guess we could go to urgent care and get it looked at."

He nodded triumphantly. "Good choice. I'll go get my car. Don't move."

He drove her to urgent care, and she got her ankle x-rayed. Just a sprain, like she'd thought. She was right. Gavin was wrong. The doctor wrapped her ankle, gave her crutches to use, and told her to stay off of it and elevate it.

She clumped back out into the waiting room on the crutches and Gavin looked up from reading a magazine. He sprung from his seat. "You okay?"

"A sprain. Like I said."

He nodded. "Let's get you home." She wasn't going to argue with him. Exhaustion flowed through her, and her muscles were starting to scream at her.

He drove her home, helped her up the porch steps, and stood beside her as she looked at the long set of stairs heading up to her apartment.

He took one look at the stairs and shook his head. "No way you're doing those on crutches. I'm carrying you."

He took her crutches, set them against the wall, and swept her up, his arms strong and steady. The warmth of his body seeped through her. She swore it warmed her to her very bones. But she resolutely ignored it.

He climbed the stairs as if her weight was nothing to him. He set her down by the door and she unlocked it. Before she could protest, he swept her up in his arms again and carried her inside, her head resting on his shoulder.

He strode over to the couch and gently set her down, then grabbed a pillow and placed it under her foot.

"I'll go get your crutches." He returned with them and set them near her. "Now, you need more ice. You got plastic bags or an ice pack?"

"No ice pack, but the bags are in the drawer to the left of the fridge."

She settled against the plush pillows on her couch, reveling in their comfort, glad to finally rest. He returned with the ice bag and placed it on her ankle.

"Thank you for all your help. I do appreciate it."

He nodded, not saying anything.

"I'll be fine now."

He nodded again.

"I mean… it's okay for you to go now." Did she have to spell it out to him?

"I'm staying."

"Gavin, you don't need to do that."

"Yep, I do. I'm going to make sure you stay off that foot. And I'll make you some dinner. You got anything to cook?"

"You don't have to do all that. I'm fine."

"So you said."

"I'm not sure what I have. I haven't made it to the grocery store yet."

"I'll find something."

He headed to the kitchen, and she closed her eyes. There was really no arguing with the man. Sounds of cabinets opening and closing and a pot clanking on the stove came from across the room.

She grabbed her tablet from the table and browsed through the entertainment news. She might not be performing now, but she still liked to know who was getting what roles. She smiled in delight when she saw her niece, Chloe, had snagged a leading role in an off-Broadway show. Guilt tugged at her for the choices she'd made, but at least she hadn't messed up anything for her niece. Which was the whole point of her choice. She wasn't going to tank anyone else's career with her decisions.

Gavin came back and handed her a bowl. "You're right. You didn't have much. But I found some pasta and bacon. Made some pasta carbonara."

She took the bowl and tried a bite. "It's delicious."

"Thanks."

He sat in a chair near her, eating a bowl of his own. The room started to darken with the evening.

The day finally took its toll, and she set the bowl on the table. She should probably keep up a nice conversation with Gavin, but exhaustion crept in. She'd just close her eyes for a moment.

When she opened her eyes again, early morning light was filtering through the window. Had she spent the whole night on the couch? She pushed herself up to a sitting position, wincing slightly as she moved her foot.

She'd had the strangest dream about Gavin. He had been standing over her, adjusting the throw around her, and pushing a lock of her hair away from her face. And she'd had the strongest feeling that he wanted to kiss her. She stretched her arms and blinked her eyes, slowly waking up, chasing away any remnants of the dream.

Her mouth dropped open when she looked across the room and saw Gavin sleeping in the most uncomfortable position ever in the chair by the window. He'd spent the night?

She reached for her crutches and cringed when one went crashing to the floor. Gavin sprung from the chair. "You okay?"

"Yes, I'm sorry. I knocked over one of the crutches."

He nodded and scrubbed his hands over his face. "Okay, let me help you up."

He came over, handed her the crutches, and watched her carefully as she swung through them.

"I'm going to go get cleaned up. Get ready for work."

"You got coffee in this place?"

"I do."

"I'll make us some while you get ready. Then I'll drive you to the theater. *If* you promise to stay off that foot."

The way her foot was throbbing this morning, he wasn't asking much of her. The thought of walking made her shiver. "Thank you, Gavin. You've done so much for me. You didn't need to stay all night."

"It was nothing." He stepped back, letting her pass. She could feel his gaze on her as she headed down the hallway.

She changed and got ready—it took longer than she thought it would. Who knew how awkward it was to do every little thing when you were on crutches? She clumped back into the main room. Gavin was standing by the window, sipping coffee. She maneuvered over by him.

"Your coffee is there on the table. Why don't you sit while you drink it?"

"It's getting kind of late." Wasn't he the one always commenting if she wasn't at the theater first thing each morning?

"We have time for coffee," he countered.

She lowered herself onto the chair and took a sip. A few minutes wouldn't make much difference.

Gavin leaned against the wall by the window, staring outside toward the water. A peaceful silence settled between them.

"I reconsidered, and I think you should stay home today. Stay off that foot."

The peace was shattered. "I have work to do. I'll be fine."

"You're a stubborn one, aren't you?"

"I am. And if you haven't noticed, I don't like being told what to do."

He tossed her a lazy grin. "Oh, I've noticed."

She set down her cup and pushed up out of the chair. "We should go."

They headed to the door, and he paused, eyeing her. She shook her head. "You are not carrying me down those stairs."

"Okay, then give me one of your crutches. You hang onto the railing with one hand and use the crutch with your other. I'll walk right in front of you to make sure you don't fall."

She did as he suggested and the first few steps were awkward, but she started to get the hang of it by the time she'd gone down all the steps. He drove her to the theater and followed her back to her office. He was like her constant shadow. It annoyed her…

… and comforted her.

He got her settled onto her chair, setting her crutches within reach. "You all set? I've got to check in at The Bike Shop. Will you be okay?"

"I'll be fine." How many times did she have to tell him that?

"Okay, I'll be back to check on you. How about I bring you lunch?" He held up a hand. "And don't even try to tell me that I don't have to do that. Because I want to."

"Then, thank you. I appreciate it."

He turned and walked across the room with one last look back at her before he left.

Silence thundered around her. But she ignored it. She had work to do.

CHAPTER 16

They fell into an easy rhythm over the next few days. Gavin came to get her each morning and drove her to the theater. He picked up lunch for them. They grabbed dinner out a few times. And he'd drive her home and make sure she got safely up her stairs. By the seventh day, she was willing to give up the crutches. The ankle was a bit sore and throbbed a little if she overdid it, but it was healing.

She sat at her desk with her notebook, checking off her list. The dress rehearsals were booked. The sound system had finally been checked out, and it was ready to go. The programs were at the printer and would be delivered soon. She had a large poster placed in the outside window announcing the grand opening. Tickets were on sale online now, and soon she'd hire someone to work at the physical ticket counter. Beverly had recommended a few people that she could interview.

A phone rang, and she frowned until she remembered she'd had the theater's phone line put back into service. She shoved some papers around on her desk and uncovered the phone. "Hello, Magnolia Key Theater."

"Yes, hello. This is Felicity Moore from Southwest Florida Life magazine. May I speak to Tori Duran?"

"This is she."

"I'm the head of the entertainment section. I heard you bought the theater and you're reopening it. I'd love to set up a time to interview you."

She swallowed hard as her heart skipped in her chest and she fought back a rising panic. "I… uh…" An interview was the last thing in the world she wanted right now. But… it would be good for publicity. And they needed that.

"I'd like to come get some photos before the opening, then come get some more on your opening night."

She battled with her needs and the theater's needs. She let out a sigh as the theater won.

"Okay, that would be fine," she said, hoping her voice didn't betray the battle raging inside her.

"Can we do it later this week? Would Friday morning work for you?"

"Yes, that would work."

"Okay, Tori, I'll see you Friday."

She hung up the phone as her heart ricocheted in her chest, and a feeling of impending doom pressed down on her like this morning's fog that had rolled in from the gulf. But it would be okay, she promised herself. She looked nothing like she used to. No one would figure it out. She looked nothing like Victoria Duran anymore. Victoria had been replaced by Tori, a woman who could walk through the world unnoticed. Or at least she hoped she could.

She shuffled the papers on her desk, organizing them into neat piles. Tidy. Predictable. Routine. That's how she wanted her life to be now. But if she wanted the theater to be successful, she'd need to get publicity, something she'd been avoiding. But this was one little interview. It would be okay. And there she was, assuring herself she'd be fine just like she was always assuring Gavin. And she didn't think she believed herself any more than Gavin had believed her.

Tori chose her outfit with deliberate care Friday morning—a plain, simple outfit— assuring her reflection in the mirror that she looked nothing like her former self. She pulled her hair back with a hairband and barely touched her face with makeup. She would be fine…

Gavin was busy at The Bike Shop this morning, so she drove herself over to the theater, checking her watch time and again. Dreading the interview and yet wanting it to happen so it would be over.

A young woman with dark brown hair and a quick smile walked through the open door and into the lobby. "Miss Duran? Hi, I'm Felicity Moore."

"Hi, call me Tori." *It was safer.* She reached out and shook the woman's hand.

"Tori, I appreciate you taking the time to talk to me. When I heard you were renovating the theater and reopening it, I was thrilled. I used to come here to the productions when I was younger. Back before they closed it. It's great that it's opening up again."

"How about I show you around?" Tori led her through the lobby and into the main theater. She showed her the stage and the backstage area, and all the while, Felicity peppered her with questions. They ended up back in her office, and Felicity took a seat across from her.

"You've done a great job. It looks just like it used to, only…" Felicity laughed. "A bit more spruced up. It was really showing its age and needed work by the time it closed."

"I am proud of how it turned out."

"So, what made you decide to purchase the theater?"

She searched for an answer to give, something that kept her far away from her former life on stage. "Just like you, I used to come to the theater. It was with my grandmother when I was a young girl. We'd come to Magnolia Key each summer, and coming to the theater productions was the highlight of each trip."

"Ah, I see. And are you staying here, or are you just here for the renovations and opening?"

Good question. Was she going to stay here? She wanted to, but still hadn't decided. She still felt like an outsider. "I'm not certain." Might as well tell the truth.

She looked up at the sound of Gavin at the door. "Gavin, come in. Meet Felicity Moore from Southwest Florida Life magazine." She turned to Felicity. "Gavin is helping with the restoration."

Felicity turned to him, smiling warmly. "Oh, could I interview you too?"

"No," he said abruptly, his face hardening into an icy stare.

Felicity's eyes widened, startled, but she nodded. "Okay, then. I'll just talk to Miss Duran —I mean, Tori."

Tori stood up. "Can you give me a minute?" She headed to the doorway, pushing Gavin out into the hallway. "Why are you being so rude? Would it hurt you to talk to her?"

"Yes."

"Yes, you'll talk to her?"

"No, I will not talk to her."

"Gavin, why are you being so... strange?" The icy look on his features remained unthawed.

"I can't believe you'd have the media come here." His words came out clipped and angry.

"We need the publicity."

"Not all publicity is good publicity." He growled the words.

Well, she knew that better than most. But she was putting her fears aside to help the theater.

"You shouldn't have called them. Do you really need to parade around and get all this recognition for renovating the theater? I thought you were doing it because you *cared* about the theater." His eyes flashed.

"I do care about it," she shot back at him.

"You should stop the interview and ask her to leave."

"I'm not going to do that. I want people to know the theater is opening." *And quit telling me what to do.*

"Don't blame me if it doesn't turn out like you want it to." He spun around and headed down the hallway, his angry footsteps echoing and bouncing off the walls.

Confusion swirled through her, mixed with a growing resentment. She was getting tired of his moods. Of his opinions. Of him telling her what to do.

Enough of Gavin. She had a theater to run. She headed back into her office to finish the interview.

CHAPTER 17

Anger throbbed through Gavin as he strode down the sunny, palm-lined street. The bright day mocked his stormy fury. Why on earth had Tori agreed to do that interview? Was she just looking for attention? Need recognition for all she'd done? It wasn't going to turn out well, he was certain. He strode into Coastal Coffee, the familiar scent of roasted coffee beans and yeasty cinnamon rolls temporarily soothing his frazzled nerves.

Miss Eleanor was sitting at a table at the far side of the room. Before he could turn around and sneak back out the door, she looked up and saw him. She waved him over with a brisk motion. And it was more of a command than an invitation. He threaded through the tables until he reached hers.

"Morning, Miss Eleanor."

She folded her paper with an audible crinkling of pages and set it neatly to the side. "Good morning, Gavin. Have a seat." Once again, more of a command.

He dropped heavily into the seat across from her. Beverly stopped by the table. "Coffee?"

"Yes, please. And—" He glanced at the chalkboard over the counter with the day's offerings. "A cinnamon roll. No, make that two rolls." He was pretty sure it would take a double load of cinnamon rolls to abate his annoyance.

Beverly poured steaming black coffee into the mug in front of him and headed off to get his order. Miss Eleanor peered intently at him over the rim of her glasses. "What's wrong? Something going wrong with the restoration?"

"No, why do you ask?"

"Because you look like you want to throttle someone." She pinned him with a look that he couldn't avoid.

He exhaled deeply. "No, the renovations went well. Things are coming along for the grand opening."

"Then what's the problem?"

"It's just…" He shrugged. "Tori is talking to a reporter. And she wanted me to."

"Ah… so that's it." She nodded. "But you can't let what happened before cloud your judgment. It was just a… misunderstanding. And most people in town believe you now, don't they?"

"Some," he admitted grudgingly. "But that wasn't the only time the media upended my life."

Miss Eleanor double-tapped her fingers on the table. "So, are you going to tell me what happened the other time?"

He couldn't believe he was even considering telling Miss Eleanor, of all people. She knew everything about everyone on the island. But this was one thing he wasn't keen on sharing.

"Well?" she prodded, cocking her head, staring at him with a look he couldn't ignore.

Taking a deep breath, he dove in. "It was when I was away from the island. I lived in Los Angeles."

She nodded, her eyes softening slightly to encourage him to continue.

"I was… uh… romantically involved with this actress, Anna. Things were going great for us. Then a movie she was in hit it big at the box office. There was a whirlwind of parties and galas and interviews. And one of the tabloids started a baseless rumor that I was going to ask Anna to marry me."

"And were you?"

"No." He paused, collecting his thoughts. "Anna changed when she hit the big times. The woman I'd fallen for disappeared under all the glitz and glamour."

He set his elbows on the table, leaning into the memory, then quickly snatched them back when he saw Miss Eleanor's disapproving gaze shift to his elbows. "I came to realize I didn't even really like her anymore. She became self-centered and demanding. Treated people horribly, like they were beneath her. She insisted I attend all these events with her. Dictated what I should wear. Kept acting like we were an item even though I'd told her that I didn't feel like things were working out for us."

"Anyway, it all blew up at a big party for her birthday. It was crowded with actors and producers and so many journalists milling about. It was like the who's who of Hollywood had all turned out for this big gala. And then some reporter called out, asking if tonight was the night I was going to get down on one knee and ask Anna to marry me. The crowd went silent and everyone turned to stare at me. I was shocked. Stunned. Anna's eyes lit up expectantly, and she had a... smug smile on her lips. And... well, it didn't go well from there. Her smile faded as I stood there, not saying a word, and certainly not going down on one knee. She snatched a glass from a passing waiter and I ended up with a glass of champagne tossed in my face. She stomped off, embarrassed. I did feel a twinge of regret that she was embarrassed like that, but I couldn't ask her to marry me just because the media thought I should."

"No, you couldn't."

"It was like the media would just make up their own version of my world. That's what they do." He sighed wearily. "They twist their narrative to make a story."

Miss Eleanor leaned forward and touched his hand. "Yes, sometimes the media can cause trouble. And I don't blame you for wanting to avoid them. But... don't you think that Tori is doing the interview to get some publicity for the theater? Not for herself?"

He frowned, considering her words. "I honestly don't know. Maybe I did mix up my feelings about Anna and her always wanting media attention with Tori's motivation."

"Yes, I think you did. Tori doesn't strike me as a woman who craves attention. She's level-headed. And a hard worker. I peeked in the theater the other day while the workmen were there and it really has turned out nicely. She's done a wonderful job. And I appreciate you overseeing it and making sure it was restored back to how it was."

He nodded. It was true. Tori had poured her heart and soul into the theater. "To be honest, that was mostly Tori's doing. She's organized and demanded exceptional work from everyone involved in the restoration. She's got things planned for the grand opening. It's all her. All I did was help."

Miss Eleanor eyed him for a moment, as if she could see right through him. "So you admire her?"

A crease formed on his forehead. "Yes."

"And you have a fondness for her." It was a statement, not a question.

"Sure, I like her."

Her gaze didn't waver. "And did you storm out of the theater like you came raging in here?"

A self-deprecating smile tugged at his lips. "I might have. It might have been a dramatic exit, fitting for a theater."

Her eyes twinkled with amusement. "Then I presume you're going to head back and apologize?"

He laughed, his anger starting to abate. "Yes, I do believe I'll head back there and apologize. I'm afraid I let my past color my perception of the current situation."

CHAPTER 18

Tori's annoyance was starting to move from a rolling boil to a simmer. Maybe.

Gavin and his opinions and attitude were too much to take sometimes. She yanked open the desk drawer and grabbed a pen, contemplating throwing it across the room in frustration. Instead, she dropped it on the desk, and it clattered and rolled across the surface.

She grabbed her purse, pulled out a key, and unlocked the bottom desk drawer. She took the pendant out and stared at it, wondering what secrets it held. Why had someone hidden it in the dressing-table drawer? Her desk lamp caught one of the diamonds just right and it sparkled in appreciation, as if glad to be out of its hiding place and out in the world again.

She slipped the chain around her neck and fastened it, fingering the pendant as it rested on her chest. Who wore this before her?

"Hi." Gavin's voice startled her. Again. Why did he always do that?

He moved through the door with tentative steps.

"What do you want?" She knew her voice sounded impatient and annoyed because… well, she *was* impatient and annoyed with him.

He crossed over and stood at the other side of the desk, staring at the pendant for a moment before raising his eyes to hers. "I just came to… to apologize."

"Really?"

"Yes, I'm afraid I overreacted."

"You think?" She rolled her eyes.

"I just didn't want to talk to anyone from the press." He shifted his weight from foot to foot.

"You made yourself perfectly clear."

"I'm sorry I jumped to conclusions."

A look of contrition hovered in his eyes.

But this time, she wasn't buying it. Wasn't willing to be appeased. It still stung deeply that he'd accused her of doing this all for some kind of attention. Personal attention was the last thing in the world she wanted. Did he not know her at all after all this time working together?

She glared at him, anger simmering just below the surface. Did he think a half apology would change anything? "Gavin, you're impossible to be around. You're hot and cold. Caring and icy. You're always pressing your opinions on me. Telling me what I should or shouldn't do. And I frankly don't have the energy to deal with your moods anymore. I have things that need to be done. The grand opening is near. I can't waste time worrying or dealing with your ever-changing moods."

"I really am sorry." His words were soft and sincere.

"Fine. I accept your apology." Though she really didn't. His words still stung. Deeply. Like he'd accused her of being some kind of diva. The furthest thing in the world from who she was now.

"So things are… okay? Between us, I mean?" His expression looked hopeful.

"Sure. We can be colleagues. But only because Miss Eleanor insisted. Once the theater is up and running, I hope… I hope you can just stay far away from me."

Hurt flickered in his eyes and just as quickly disappeared. "If that's what you want."

"It is." She nodded firmly, steeling her resolve.

He stared at her for a long moment, then turned and disappeared out the door. Her triumph for taking a stand was short-lived as his footsteps echoed down the hall. She slumped in her chair. But she'd done the right thing by sending him away. Now maybe he'd leave her in peace to get the theater up and going. He could go back to his bike shop and annoy people there. Sit by himself and brood at the counter at Sharky's.

She didn't need his help. Didn't want it.

Still, she sat at her desk, fingering the pendant and staring at the empty doorway.

Tori saw no sign of Gavin for days. Which was exactly what she wanted, right? The question echoed through her mind. Growing more uncertain with each repetition. Was it really what she wanted? She did catch herself thinking she needed to tell him this or ask him that as the days went on. His absence had opened up a void she hadn't known existed.

But it was better this way, she tried to convince herself. She didn't have to worry about what kind of mood he'd be in. Or listen to his opinions. Or be accused of something she hadn't done. Still, the theater felt empty without him.

She grabbed her bike and headed over to Coastal Coffee for breakfast before going into work. She found herself in need of company. She'd been used to the workers, and then Gavin always being around at the theater. Now, the emptiness clung to every aisle, every seat in the vast theater.

Dress rehearsals began next week, and the theater would once again be alive with activity, but this week had been filled with unwelcome silence and a loneliness she couldn't shake.

She pushed into the cafe, and the welcome aroma of fresh coffee and baked goods surrounded her like a friendly embrace. The murmur of voices and clatter of ceramic cups were a sharp contrast to the silence of the theater and a mocking reminder of her solitude.

Beverly waved to her as she took a table and

soon came over with a pot of coffee. "Coffee, yes?"

"Yes, please." She moved her cup closer to Beverly.

"You haven't been in here for a bit." Beverly's eyes held a hint of concern.

A concern that warmed Tori's heart. She was making friends here on Magnolia, ones who noticed when she wasn't around. It made her feel more like she was becoming a part of the town. "I've just been busy with the theater."

"I saw the posters up. I've bought my ticket for opening night."

Pride swelled through her. "You did?" A surge of gratitude swept through her at her friend's support.

"Of course. Wouldn't miss it. Gavin has been in here and just about every other business in town putting up posters."

Miss Eleanor approached the table, joining their conversation. "Yes, Gavin has been busy promoting the theater."

"He has?" She couldn't hide her surprise.

"Yes. He seems pretty proud of all you've accomplished." Miss Eleanor gave a brief bob of her head.

She doubted that. "I'm surprised he's

putting out the posters. We had a bit of an... argument. I did an interview with a reporter about the theater and how it was opening again. Gavin accused me of seeking the limelight. Wanting attention. Said I shouldn't talk to the reporter. That I'd regret it, which really makes no sense. But honestly, I just wanted some free publicity for the theater. He was totally overreacting. And his accusation—it—it hurt."

Miss Eleanor tilted her head. "And did he apologize?"

"He tried to, but I didn't really listen to him. He's moody and I never know which Gavin I'm going to see. The nice, helpful one or the grumpy, opinionated one. I just wanted to be left alone to finish everything that needs to be done before the opening."

"Gavin is a good man. He's just had some trouble in his life with the media." Eleanor motioned to an empty chair. "Do you mind?"

"Please, take a seat."

"Gavin is... not a fan of anyone in the media. Reporters, magazines, papers. He... ah..." Beverly set down the coffeepot on the table. "Gavin had a rough time with the press here in Magnolia."

"What happened?" She frowned.

"He made some remarks about the lighthouse when a reporter came to cover the renovations. They twisted what he said. They twisted it into saying he was against the restoration and against tourism and growth of the town. A lot of the townsfolk shunned him." Beverly shrugged. "So he has a healthy distrust of the media."

Miss Eleanor frowned in disapproval. "I stood up for him, though. That article was pure rubbish. Gavin loves the town and is totally invested in preserving its heritage along with making sure the town still thrives." She defended him staunchly.

"I guess I can see how that would make him distrust the media. It's too bad his words were twisted like that."

Eleanor nodded emphatically. "Indeed. I defended him. Even wrote a letter to the editor. But the damage was done, and it took a long time for some of the townspeople to come around."

"Gavin is a proud man, and he hasn't quite forgiven the media for what they did," Beverly added.

Miss Eleanor nodded and continued, "And I'll not talk out of turn, but he had another run-in with them when he lived in Los Angeles. He has good reason not to trust them."

Guilt crept through her at how she'd shut down his apology and thrown him out of the theater. The theater where he'd been such a help with the restorations.

Now, after hearing Miss Eleanor and Beverly's truth about Gavin's past, she saw his actions in a new light. "I didn't know any of this."

"Now you do," Miss Eleanor said as she rose from her seat. "So what are you going to do about it?"

"I'm not sure."

"You'll go talk to him." It was more of a command than a suggestion. "Just don't let him shut you out." Miss Eleanor turned and headed over to her regular table.

Beverly picked up the coffeepot. "He's a good man, and I'm sure he didn't mean to hurt your feelings. To accuse you of looking for accolades or anything like that. He's just…"

"Distrustful of the media. I see that now." She owed him an apology, at the very least. Maybe she could even salvage some of their friendship.

Beverly gave her a warm smile. "I hope you two can work things out."

"I do too." And she realized she really meant it. She'd missed Gavin since their argument. She missed sharing her day with him. Telling him what was going on at the theater. Their meals at Sharky's. All of it.

CHAPTER 19

Tori headed straight to The Bike Shop. Miss Eleanor was right. She needed to try and work things out with Gavin. She'd had no idea of his past run-ins with the media. But it still stung a bit that he'd accused her of doing the interview for her own personal gain. That simply was not true.

The door was propped open to the shop, and she stepped inside tentatively, taking a moment to let her eyes adjust to the dimmer lighting. Gavin crouched in the far corner, focused intently on a bike he was working on. She took a deep, steadying breath and crossed the concrete floor.

"Hey," she said softly when she reached him.

His head jerked up, his eyes widening in surprise. He grabbed a rag, wiped the grease from his hand, and stood to face her. "Didn't expect to see you here. Are you having problems with your bike?"

"No, it's not the bike." She wiped her palms on her thighs. "I... I wanted to talk to you. Apologize."

He cocked one eyebrow.

"I didn't really give you a chance when you came to apologize to me. I just sent you away. I'm really, really sorry." She met his gaze, hoping he could see the sincerity in her eyes.

He eyed her closely, a frown wrinkling his forehead. "What changed?"

Honesty was the best way, she reminded herself. "I heard about what happened with the lighthouse restoration. How your words were twisted in that article and a lot of the town turned against you."

His eyes narrowed. "Who told you about that?"

"Miss Eleanor and Beverly. But don't be mad at them. I'm glad I know. I understand better why you didn't want to talk to Felicity. You had no reason to trust her."

"I don't trust her or any reporter," he said emphatically.

"Oh, I think she's a nice woman. I'm hoping she'll do a good job on her article. We can use the publicity."

He looked doubtful. "But I am sorry, though, that I accused you of wanting attention. I realize you were doing it for the theater."

"I was hurt, I admit. I just couldn't believe you'd think that about me after all the time we spent together." She had trusted him, considered him a friend. But his accusation hurt.

"I know. I was wrong. I'm sorry." He apologized again.

"I'm sorry, too. So, will you accept my apology?" She looked at him imploringly, wanting nothing more than to get back on good footing with him. She'd come to realize his friendship meant a lot to her.

"I accept." He started to reach out for her hand, then pulled back, grinning. "But I guess you don't want to shake on it. Not with this greasy hand."

A smile slipped across her lips. "Probably not. So we're all good now?"

"We are." His words were firm and full of assurance.

The last of her doubt and her hurt faded away. Relief surged through her. "That's great. So... are you going to start coming by the theater again? I've missed you."

"Ah, you have projects for me, do you?" His teasing smile made her grin again.

"I might have a few." She looked around the shop. "But if you're busy with The Bike Shop, I understand."

"I've got plenty of time. Jonny can run the shop."

"The rehearsals start this week. I can't wait to see if this all comes together like I planned."

"I'm sure it will. I have faith in you."

His words made her heart soar.

"Let me get cleaned up, and I'll meet you over at the theater in a bit."

"That would be nice." It would be great. Fabulous, actually. A smile etched its way onto her face, and she wasn't sure when it might go away. She turned and walked out into the warm sunshine.

With each pedal of her bike, her spirits rose. Gavin was back working on the theater and the opening. And they were back to being friends. All was right with her world.

She slowed her speed for a moment and frowned, her eyebrows knitting together. She probably should have been honest with Gavin and told him about her past as a Broadway actress. But they had just made a tenuous connection again, and she didn't want to do anything to jeopardize that. Plenty of time to tell him after the opening. She would tell him everything then, she silently promised herself.

Gavin scrubbed the grease from his hands and went by his home to change into a clean shirt. A lightness hovered over him now that he and Tori were speaking again. If she had given him a chance, he would have told her himself about the lighthouse restoration article. He shook his head ruefully. No, in all honesty, he probably wouldn't have. It wasn't something he ever talked about. Just like the media and Anna. Some things were better left unsaid and buried in the past.

He'd been mad when Tori had just sent him

away, but he realized he'd hurt her feelings when he rushed to judge her.

Being friends with a woman like Tori was complicated. But hopefully, they were back on track.

He walked over to the theater and climbed the front steps lined with glass cases with posters proclaiming the grand opening. As he entered the lobby, excitement thrummed through him to be involved with the opening once again.

He found Tori in her office. "I'm here."

She looked up, and her eyes twinkled with welcome. "Great." She stood, picked up her notebook, and walked over to him. "Let's get started."

Her notebook. He'd missed that. The way she organized everything.

"Let's start." He stepped aside to let her through the doorway. As she brushed past him, it felt like all the air was sucked out of him. *What was that all about?*

Ignoring it, he followed her down the hallway. They spent the day working through her list. Getting things ready. Double-checking the sound system and the lights. Finally, she collapsed on a front-row seat. "I'm beat."

"Bit tired myself." He lowered himself to sit

next to her. Their arms brushed against each other on the armrest. He stared down at them for a moment, then looked up at her. "I think we're ready for the rehearsals though, don't you?"

"I hope so."

"How about I walk you home?"

"I've got my bike."

"Okay, how about I walk you home and we walk your bike with us?" He grinned at her.

They locked up the theater and headed outside. He took the bike and rolled it beside them as they walked. When they got to her apartment, he couldn't help but recall how it had felt to carry her up the stairs in his arms. He could almost feel her there.

He dismissed the thought as she opened the door. "You want to come in and have a drink?"

"Sure would." He stepped inside, glad to have a chance to spend more time with her. He'd missed her these last days. Missed her smile. Missed teasing her. Missed... well, everything about her.

They took a couple of beers and went out on her balcony, settling onto a pair of comfortable chairs.

"It was nice being back at the theater," he said.

She turned to him and smiled. "It was nice having you back."

His heartbeat quickened at her smile and he had to keep from dropping his mouth open in surprise. Was he falling for this woman? He'd sworn off women after the whole Anna episode.

But Tori was so different than Anna. She didn't seek out the spotlight. She was just a normal person, like him. He tried to sort out his feelings as they sat and chatted about the grand opening. Her eyes sparkled when she talked about it, full of excitement.

"You've done a remarkable job with all of this. I don't know how you figured out so much about booking in a traveling troupe of actors, and so much about lighting and everything, but I'm impressed."

A look of momentary *something* crossed her face before she smiled gently. "I'm just glad it's all working out."

He rose. "I should go. I still need to run by the shop and see if Jonny got that bike I was working on finished."

She stood. "I didn't mean to monopolize your time."

"Oh, you didn't. Not at all. I enjoyed working at the theater… and this nice break this evening."

They headed inside, and she walked him to the door. They stood there facing each other, and he had the strongest urge to… kiss her. He blinked twice, surprised by the thought. *Kiss her?*

He cleared his throat. "I… I was wondering if you'd…" Get your words out, man. "Would you like to go out to dinner with me? Like a… date?"

Her eyes widened in surprise. "A date?" It was barely a whisper.

"Yes." He nodded, holding his breath, waiting for her answer.

"You think that's a good idea since we're working together again?"

He chewed his lip. He hadn't considered that. "Yes, I think it would be okay. Don't you? We seem to be getting along fine now. And… I'd like to take you out."

She stared at him for a moment, and he swore her gaze dropped to his lips before meeting his eyes again. "Okay, that sounds nice."

"Tomorrow night work?"

She nodded.

"I'll pick you up here at six."

"Okay."

"But I'll be by the theater tomorrow too. Don't worry." He turned and hurried down the stairs, wondering what he'd done. He'd asked Tori out on a date. How long had it been since he'd gone on a date? Had he made the right decision to ask her out? She was right, they were co-workers. But soon the opening would be over and he wouldn't have an excuse to see her so often.

Unless, of course, they were dating.

Tori closed the door softly behind Gavin and leaned against it. Gavin had asked her on a date. A date.

Was that a good idea? They had just sorted things out so they could work together. But, the thing was, she would like to date him. Even if it might not be the smartest idea.

Even as her practical side listed off all the reasons they shouldn't date, her heart stubbornly resisted.

The man fascinated her. She loved being around him. Talking to him. Even listening to his many opinions. Okay, maybe *some* of his opinions. But he had learned to listen to her counterpoints, and that was a step in the right direction. A sign they'd both grown and learned from each other.

Firmly listening to her heart, she decided to take this chance. A chance to see where things would lead them.

She wandered out onto the balcony and sat down, staring across the shimmering turquoise water. The sun painted the sky with fiery tones of orange and yellow. She took a deep breath of the salty air, feeling the tension in her shoulders fade. As the sun glided below the horizon, she let her regrets about her past and her fears slip away with it.

So much had changed since she'd come to Magnolia Key. After her disastrous and unexpected last night on the stage, she'd needed a place to escape. A place where no one knew her. She was starting to believe she could put her whole past behind her here in Magnolia.

Working with the theater fed her soul. Gave her purpose. If she couldn't be on stage anymore, at least she could provide the stage for other actors. While her life used to be firmly entrenched in the spotlight, now all she craved was for the Magnolia Theater to be a success.

A gentle breeze blew her hair, and she swept it out of her eyes, watching the waves roll constantly to shore in a slow, soothing motion.

She finally had found peace here on Magnolia Key. A peace that she'd thought she'd lost forever.

CHAPTER 20

A knock sounded at her door and Tori hurried over to answer it, smoothing her hair and straightening her dress in anticipation. Gavin stood there looking relaxed and casual. If he was as nervous as she was, there was no sign of it. His hair was still damp from a recent shower, the ends curling slightly in a way that made her heart skip a beat. Khaki shorts showed off his long, tanned legs, and a button-down shirt with rolled-up sleeves exposed his strong forearms. She was glad he'd told her semi casual. The simple teal t-shirt dress she'd picked was a perfect match for his outfit.

They headed out, and he paused on the porch. "You mind walking?"

"Not at all. Where are we going?"

"You'll see," he said with a hint of playful secrecy.

She followed him along the sidewalk until he cut across at the far end of the island. He slipped off his shoes at the edge of the beach. She did the same, enjoying the cool feel of the sand beneath her feet. He took her hand, leading her across the beach. As they went around the bend, she gasped.

A wispy white canopy fluttered in the ocean breeze. Beneath it, a cozy blanket and smattering of cushions beckoned. Two lanterns flickered beside the blanket, casting a warm, romantic glow. A small, low table was centered under the canopy, adorned with a vase bursting with bright flowers. A wine bucket rested beside the table and a wicker basket sat to one side.

She clapped her hands in delight. "Gavin, it's wonderful."

His mouth spread into a wide, satisfied grin. "I was hoping you'd like it."

"You did all this?" Her voice filled with awe as she stared at the magical setup.

He laughed. "No, but I arranged it. There's a fledgling business start-up that's trying to gain more customers here on Magnolia Key. I heard about them and hired them to do all this. Thought it might give their business a boost. They took photos of the setup to use for their promo."

He led her over to the blanket, and they ducked under the canopy. She sank down on the plush cushions and he dropped down beside her, close but not quite touching. "Champagne?" he asked, reaching for the bottle nestled in the ice bucket.

She nodded, and he poured two flutes. He raised his. "To our first official date."

Her heart skipped a beat. "To our date." First? Did that mean he planned on more? She took a sip of the pale yellow liquid, the bubbles dancing across her tongue. "This is nice."

"It is." Though he was looking right at her, not at his champagne, and his meaning was crystal clear.

He opened the basket and spread out the food. Strawberries, cheese, crackers, a veggie plate and dip, along with a platter with an assortment of delicious-looking desserts. "Think there will be enough?" he teased.

"I think so." She grinned back at his infectious smile.

They savored their meal and their time

together as the sun sank lower in the sky. He finally stood and reached down a hand. "One more thing."

She took his hand and stood as he reached into the basket, pulled out a small speaker, and connected it to his phone. He turned on some music. The soft melody drifted across the sand, melding with the gentle sound of the waves. "Dance?"

She nodded and stepped into his arms. He held her close as they swayed to the music. In his arms, she felt a warmth sink through her to her very bones. A welcome warmth full of hope that in turn filled her with contentment. The stars began to twinkle above them in the darkening sky. The sun gave one last burst of brilliant color before sinking below the horizon, throwing streaks of orange that danced with the fluffy clouds.

She rested her cheek against his chest and listened to his heartbeat. It thumped jaggedly, just like hers. He pulled her closer. Still, they swayed gently to the music, the waves, the night breeze. He finally stepped back and tilted her chin up, his gaze locking with hers.

Time stood still. Her breath caught and

there was no force of nature strong enough to break their gazes. He lowered his lips to hers and kissed her gently. A small sigh escaped her lips, unbidden but unstoppable.

"That was nice," he murmured as he pulled back slightly.

"Hmm," was all she could manage to say, still lost in the magic of the moment.

"We should practice to see if we could do it better."

She sincerely doubted they could, but she sure was willing to give it a try. He kissed her again. Then they were dancing and kissing and laughing and talking as the night sky grew dark and the moon played hide and seek with the clouds.

Reluctantly, he looked at his watch. "I think we're going to have to wrap this up. The company I hired is scheduled to come collect all this in just a few minutes."

A pang of disappointment crept through her. She wasn't ready for the magic to end.

He gave her one more lingering kiss and took her hand. They walked over to the blanket and each had a final sip of champagne before heading across the sand. They slipped on their shoes when they reached the sidewalk, but then he took her hand in his, not letting go. Which was fine with her because she wasn't ready to lose this connection with him. Wasn't ready for the magic to end.

As he walked her home, her heart sang in her chest. Gavin had kissed her. *Gavin had kissed her.*

When they got to her house, he stood with her on the front porch, a silly grin on his face. She probably looked the same way.

"I had a wonderful time tonight, Tori."

"I did too."

Then his face got serious. "But there's something I've been wanting to explain to you. About why I overreacted to that reporter you talked to."

She looked up, watching his face closely. "Okay, tell me."

"You see, I dated this woman. Anna. For quite a while, actually. She was an actress."

Her heart skipped a beat at his words, but she kept her expression calm.

"She only had minor roles when I first met her, but then she was in a big box-office smash hit and things changed. She changed. She always wanted attention. Always looking for the limelight. People treated her like she was special, and she treated others like… well, like she was better than they were. We grew apart, but some reporter started the rumor I was going to ask her to marry me." He looked down at her quickly. "I wasn't."

She held her breath, letting him continue.

"But everything blew up at this big party. A reporter shouted out, asking if that night was the night that I'd finally ask her to marry me. It didn't end well…" He glanced out into the night, then back toward her. "So you can see why that run-in with the media plus what happened with the lighthouse restoration… Well, I have a healthy distrust of the media."

"I can see why." She got the words out, but just barely.

"So, I promised myself I'd never date anyone who needed the spotlight like that. No one who would attract media attention. But then I met you, and now I don't have to worry about that." He smiled at her.

Her heart plunged. Oblivious to her thoughts, he leaned in and kissed her again, and her arms threaded themselves around his neck, holding him close. He finally stepped back, and she reluctantly slid her hands to her sides.

"Night, Tori."

The moment hung between them, and she was trapped between confession and wanting to preserve the fragile connection between them. Now was the time to tell him. But she couldn't. Not after what he had just told her. She'd have to find a better time. After the opening. She promised, yet again, that she'd tell him after the opening. And she'd make him understand that she wasn't like his old girlfriend.

So all she said was, "Good night." He walked down the sidewalk then turned to wave to her. She entered the apartment and walked over to the window, looking out over the water with the moonlight dancing across the waves.

She touched her lips, still feeling his kisses.

Tonight had been the most magical night of her life. Topping any opening night at the theater. And then it had all crashed down around her. She was falling for Gavin. Falling hard and fast. And at this point, she didn't even care. She didn't even try to talk herself out of it.

Tonight, Gavin Sloan had kissed her.

And then told her he'd never date someone who would attract media attention. But she didn't attract their attention anymore. She was simply Tori now.

She would tell him the truth. She would. After a successful opening, when she had time to explain. Not that she could tell him the real reason she was hiding out. But she could just say she was tired of the chaos that was Broadway. And hopefully, he'd believe her.

CHAPTER 21

Tori sat at her old wooden desk, paying bills. The opening was quickly approaching and excitement was her constant companion. The theater was alive with talking and laughing and people moving about, doing their jobs, getting everything ready. The feeling she had now was like an old friend visiting her. It was almost how she felt right before opening night, when she was still acting.

An exhilarating energy pulsed through the theater. Actors ran through their lines. Technicians tested the lights and sound system one more time. She paused her task and just soaked in the thrumming energy around her. This. This was exactly what she'd hoped for when she purchased the theater.

It was perfect. Almost perfect. She still had to tell Gavin about her stage career. But he'd understand, and they'd work things out. He understood her. Knew the person she was now. Didn't he?

She turned back to the bills, glad that soon more money would be coming in to pay for the expenses. They were sold out for opening night, though, and that thrilled her as well as humbled her. The town's support meant so much to her.

She flipped over from her bill-paying screen on her laptop to a new tab and searched for the Southwest Florida Life magazine website. She hoped the article was out and the publicity would help get people from the mainland over to see the shows like they had when she was a girl. The theater had been a big draw with cars lining up at the ferry to come over to Magnolia Key for the productions.

She found the link to the site and clicked on it. There, on the front page of the website, was the article with a large photo of the theater and… a photo of her from her last stage performance. She sat back in horror as the headline screamed her past back into plain sight for all to see.

Broadway Legend Victoria Duran's Big Comeback.

She closed her eyes briefly and drew in a big breath. She opened them again and read the whole article, word for word. Her hand trembled as she scrolled down the page. Rather than discuss the restoration of the historic theater like Felicity had implied, the article highlighted her Broadway career. Felicity had never let on that she knew her real identity. That Tori was Victoria. Never said that was the angle she was using for her article. Felicity had been so sweet and nice.

But what Felicity had done was use her to get her big scoop. Tell the world where Victoria Duran was hiding.

Tori sat back in her chair, her body tense as despair flooded through her. Her secret was out. Her safe little haven far from the lights and chaos of Broadway was gone. Now everyone would know that plain old Tori was actually Victoria Duran, star of the stage. The sheltered, quiet life she'd built for herself here on the island was shattered. She'd be back in the spotlight of unforgiving public scrutiny.

Gavin had been right to distrust Felicity and

her intentions. So very right. And she'd been so very, very wrong. She was blinded by her desire for publicity for the theater. She should have listened to his warning words instead of brushing them off so quickly and indifferently.

She had no idea how this would affect the opening. How would the people in town react to the news? She'd felt like she was just starting to belong here. Now she'd broken their trust. And what would Gavin think when he heard the truth about her past and the fact she'd hidden it from him?

The carefully crafted, safe world she'd created here on Magnolia Key exploded around her like a hurricane, leaving ruin in its wake.

She scanned the article again, taking small comfort in the fact that it didn't mention anything about the real reason she'd left the stage. At least that secret was safe and her niece, Chloe, was still protected. Unless some other reporter dug up the whole truth...

Gavin worked on the brakes on one of the rental bikes, adjusting them with practiced skill. He stood up and stretched, rubbing the kinks out of his lower back. He really should go over to the theater and see if Tori needed anything. Their date last night had been better than he'd imagined. And he could still feel the soft pressure of Tori's lips on his. And, to be honest, he'd like another kiss or two. A slight smile tugged at his lips as he shook his head wryly. Who would have thought that he would be falling for a woman again at his age and *after* he'd sworn off dating?

The creak of the front door drew his attention. Miss Eleanor walked in, looking concerned as she strode over toward him. "Gavin, we should talk."

"Miss Eleanor, what brings you here?" As far as he knew, she'd never stepped inside his shop before and was fairly certain she wasn't here to rent a bike.

"I wanted to show you something. Maybe you already know. But if not... I'd rather you hear it from me."

"What is it?" He frowned. Miss Eleanor wasn't one for dramatics, so he was concerned about the worried look in her eyes.

"The article came in Southwest Florida Life."

He frowned. "So, it wasn't flattering about

the renovations? She didn't think we did a good job? What?" He heard the defensiveness in his tone.

"Here." She pushed her phone into his hands and he stared down at the screen at the headline.

Broadway Legend Victoria Duran's Big Comeback.

He frowned when he saw the photo of someone who looked very similar to Tori. Shock hurtled through him when he enlarged it. Anger started to simmer, then boil as he confirmed it was unmistakably Tori. He scanned the article in disbelief.

Tori wasn't just Tori. She was a big-time actress on Broadway. And she'd hidden that fact from him. Even after he'd told her what happened with Anna. Or maybe because of it. He'd thought he could trust her, but he couldn't if she could keep a huge secret like this from him.

He thought back on last night. How foolish and naive he'd been. He hadn't been out on a date with Tori, he'd been on a date with her persona, the character she was playing with him.

He handed Miss Eleanor back her phone. "Thanks," he said tersely. "Appreciate finding out from you."

"So you didn't know either?" Miss Eleanor nodded slowly, her eyes searching his face. "I thought you would have told me if you knew the truth."

"Nope, I didn't know." The words hung between them like a brittle icicle. The realization that he didn't really know Tori punched him in the gut.

"I'm sorry. But this does explain a bit about why she wanted to buy the theater and restore it. Theater is her life."

"Guess so." He clenched his jaw. The theater had become his life too during the weeks he'd spent working with Tori on it. Had it all been part of her act?

"I wonder if she plans on going back to Broadway. If this was just a little break in her schedule." Miss Eleanor frowned, her forehead creasing with wrinkles. "But if she leaves, what does that mean for our theater?"

He stood there trying to hold back his anger —and his hurt. Yes, he reluctantly acknowledged that it hurt that she hadn't shared the truth about herself with him. There, he'd admitted it. "I don't know." He'd thought she cared about the theater. About its role in the town. Cared about Magnolia. Cared about him…

"I guess you should talk to her and find out. See if we have a problem on our hands. Can you do that for me?"

He nodded. "Yes. I'll find out the truth." That is, if Tori was capable of telling the truth because she sure had tricked him. She'd deceived him in a way he hadn't thought her capable of. But, evidently, she was.

Gavin stalked out of the shop after Miss Eleanor left, his thoughts ping-ponging through his mind. How could she keep something like this from him? A Broadway actress. A famous one at that, according to the article.

As he walked down the sidewalk, he steeled his heart from any memory of last night. How Tori felt in his arms. Her warm kisses. The way she looked at him in the moonlight. None of that mattered. She was an actress, for Pete's sake. She was probably acting last night. Playing a role. Passing her time while she worked on her pet project before heading back to the bright lights of the stage. Back to her adoring fans.

For all he knew, Tori had staged this whole thing as a publicity stunt. He wouldn't put anything past her. When an actress thought she was hot stuff, there was nothing she wouldn't do to keep her fame. They'd sell their very soul to get a front-page article about them. He knew that well enough from his time with Anna.

He rounded the corner, heading further down the street, and pulled up short. There, just down the block, Tori stood in what appeared to be a deep conversation with... *Cliff Griffin* of all people. Why would she...

He stepped back into the shadow of the doorway of the building he was standing in front of. Suspicion spiked through him. Tori and Cliff. His mind raced, trying to connect the dots. Did they have some kind of deal going on with the theater? Were they in this together? But then why would she have renovated it if Cliff was going to take it over? Because knowing Cliff, he would either tear down the historic building or convert it into an office building or something equally ill-suited to the needs of the town. Just like they didn't need his ridiculous high rise at the end of the boardwalk.

But clearly, Cliff must have some angle on how he could use the theater. It was all starting to make sense. Cliff used Tori to hide the fact he was eventually purchasing the theater. That must be it.

He could only hear an occasional word drifting over to him.

"I think it's a fair offer."

His eyes widened as Cliff's words reached him. He stayed in the shadows as the two of them continued to converse. Tori talked animatedly while Cliff listened and nodded. They were agreeing about something.

"It is a good offer." Tori's words reached him and he clenched his jaw, her deception cutting deep. She'd kept so many secrets. From him. From the whole town.

He turned on his heels and walked away in the opposite direction. Now was not the time to confront Tori. Oh, he would. He'd do exactly what Miss Eleanor had asked. But not until he had time to figure out exactly what she was planning to do with the theater. The real truth. Not some fabricated story like she'd made up about who she was.

There was more going on there than met the eye. He was certain of it. The two of them were up to something, and he was just the man to find out what it was and expose whatever scheme they had brewing. Because from where he was standing, it appeared she was planning on selling to Cliff.

CHAPTER 22

Tori pushed open the door to Coastal Coffee at lunchtime, the bell jingling overhead as she stepped inside. The now familiar hum of conversation and clinking of mugs went silent as she stepped inside.

A hush fell over the room. Every single person in the cafe turned to stare at her, and the heat of a blush swept across her cheeks. It seemed that news traveled quickly in a small town.

She took a deep breath. Okay, so it was apparent everyone in town had heard the news. That much was clear. She squared her shoulders and threaded her way back to the counter, ignoring the stares, and sat on a stool. Beverly stood behind the counter, silently watching her.

"So, you heard. Everyone heard." Tori didn't have to ask. She knew the answer.

Beverly pressed her lips into a thin line and nodded in silent agreement.

"I just wanted to be Tori Duran. Someone who used to come to the island. Who loved the island. I wanted to give back to Magnolia Key."

Beverly's eyes softened slightly. "Why didn't you just tell us who you were? Tell me? Tell Gavin?"

She sighed and ran her fingers along the smooth edge of the counter. "I wanted to leave that life behind me. Find peace here."

Doubt continued to linger in Beverly's eyes. "Is that really want you want?"

"Yes, really." Besides, she could never go back to Broadway after what happened. Never. And she really had no desire to now. But she did have to keep Chloe safe. Keep her from being blacklisted in the theater world. And it did happen. Often. You crossed the wrong people and your career was over.

The door popped open, and a man walked in with a camera hung around his neck. "Victoria. Victoria," he called out excitedly as he started into the cafe. "There you are. Can I have a few words from you?"

Panic started to swell up in her, and she looked helplessly at Beverly.

"I've got this." Beverly stepped out from behind the counter and intercepted the man. "You should leave."

Ignoring Beverly, the man turned and called back to Tori. "Victoria, do you plan to come back to the stage? What's your next play going to be? Your last one broke records for ticket sales."

Nash Carlisle rose from his table and walked over to the reporter. "The lady asked you nicely to leave." His tone left no room for argument.

The reporter looked from Beverly to Nash and scowled. "Fine. I'll catch her later." He turned and left.

"Thanks, Nash," Beverly said.

He nodded and sat back down at his table. Beverly returned to the counter.

"Thank you," Tori said quietly as relief washed over her.

Beverly's expression softened as she looked at Tori. "I don't know why you wanted to keep who you are a secret. Or maybe you needed to. But I do think you at least owed Gavin the truth. It's obvious that he cares about you."

Cared about her. Maybe. Past tense. Because

she wasn't certain how he was going to feel about her now. "Maybe I should have told him. And I planned to after the opening. Things were going so well between us. I just wanted to let the opening go smoothly before I rocked the boat."

"I get that. But Gavin doesn't trust easily. He's been hurt before. I'm not sure you can come back from this."

"Maybe not." What a mess she'd made of everything. And she still couldn't tell Gavin the whole truth. She couldn't risk her niece's career.

If that meant things were over with her and Gavin, then that's just the way things had to be. Because she didn't think he would understand why she did what she did unless he knew the whole truth. And that was something she couldn't tell him, even if she wanted to. She refused to put her wants over Chloe's future.

Beverly reached out and took her hand. "You're a good person, Tori," she said gently. "You've been through a lot, but you're still standing, aren't you? That takes strength and courage."

Tears threatened to spill at Beverly's support and kind words.

Beverly squeezed her hand. "You'll figure it out. I have faith in you."

Back at the theater that afternoon, the lighting technician, a young man with a head of unruly curls, knocked tentatively on her door. "Miss Duran," he began, his voice wavering slightly. "I'm sorry I didn't realize who you were. I'm such a fan of your work. I'm so honored to be working with you."

She just smiled at him and nodded. Then the lead in the play, a vibrant woman with a strong stage presence, came in gushing about working with her. Then numerous other actors in the play.

So the news was out, and everyone was treating her differently. She let out a sigh. She should head over to The Bike Shop and talk to Gavin. Get that over with. There was no use sitting here dreading their confrontation. And she was certain it would be more confrontation than conversation. She could almost picture the accusation in his eyes.

She pushed up from the desk and headed outside. As she walked along the sidewalk, people stared at her curiously. Or frowned at her. And she wasn't sure which was worse. The sunlight and gentle breeze did nothing to lift her mood. Her footsteps grew slower and slower as she neared The Bike Shop.

She took a deep breath, opened the door, and stepped inside, bracing herself for what lay ahead.

Jonny glanced up from behind the counter. "Miss Duran. Uh… hello." His eyes were wide with recognition. He stared at her. He knew.

"I'm looking for Gavin."

"Uh, ma'am. He's not here now." He fidgeted, ignoring her gaze.

"Do you know when he'll be back?" She glanced around the shop, briefly wondering if he was here and hiding from her.

"I'm not certain."

"Okay, thank you. Will you tell him I stopped by and I'm looking for him? I'd like to talk to him."

"I'll tell him, ma'am."

She headed back outside, uncertain where to go or what to do. Her whole life was in an upheaval. How did this all happen when all she had wanted was to make sure the opening of the theater was a success?

She decided to head back to the sanctuary of her apartment. At least there would be no people there. She'd be away from the prying eyes, the stares.

Well, at least until some reporter discovered where she lived. It was a small town. Everyone knew she lived here. And she was certain, for a price, someone would leak the address.

She rounded the corner to her street and peered down it. Luckily, she saw no one hanging around the house. She hurried down the street and inside, climbing the stairs to safety.

Her phone rang as she got inside, locking the door securely behind her as if that would lock out her problems. She tapped the phone and answered. "Hello?"

"Aunt Victoria, I just saw an article about you. I didn't know you'd bought a theater on Magnolia Key. Isn't that where you used to go with your grandmother when you were a girl?"

"It is." She sank onto a welcoming chair and slipped off her shoes, sinking back on the comforting cushions the held her in their embrace.

"All the news outlets have articles questioning if you're coming back to Broadway."

"No, I have no plans to."

"So you're going to live on the island?"

That had been her tentative plan. Move here permanently. Settle down. But now? With the look of distrust and unease in everyone's eyes? She just didn't know.

"I'm not really sure. But enough talk about me. Let's talk about you." She changed the subject. "I read the reviews on the play you're in. You're getting rave reviews."

"I am pleased with how it's going. This is a good stepping stone to even bigger plays."

"I'm happy for you, Chloe."

"Thanks, Aunt Victoria. I will say, I miss having you here. Going out for lunch with you at that little restaurant on the corner. Chatting about all the Broadway gossip."

The last thing she wanted was to chat about any Broadway gossip. Though, she guessed she was the current topic of most of the gossip at the moment.

"I miss you too, honey. I'll visit you." She just didn't know when, because she didn't dare show her face in New York City right now.

But hopefully, the gossip would die down. It always did. They moved on to juicer topics. Someone would sleep with someone's wife. Some couple would split. Some star would give a lackluster performance. There was always some gossip to be shared.

She sighed, knowing she had no desire to go back to that life. But what life would she have here?

She'd heard how the townspeople had stopped trusting Gavin after the media had twisted his words. What would they do to her now that they knew she had hidden her identity?

"Come visit soon, okay?"

"I'll try. Maybe we could meet somewhere? Take a little trip?"

"I'm pretty tied up with the play right now."

"Oh, I'm sure you are." There wouldn't be many breaks in Chloe's future until the play ran its course.

"Dad said to say hi if I talked to you. He was pleased you bought the theater. He remembers you talking about it when you got home from your trips there. But honestly, we both wonder why you left Broadway. You didn't even tell us that last play would be your very last one. We would have thrown a huge party. Something."

"I... I didn't want anyone to make a fuss."

That part was true, at least. She could admit that.

"Well, I have to run. I just wanted to check in with you. I hope you're at least having a good time working on the theater."

"I am." She had been. Before all this. "I'll talk to you soon, sweetie."

"Bye, Aunt Victoria."

The line went dead, and she was faced with a silent apartment. No hum and excitement like at the theater. A silence as deafening as the one when she walked into Coastal Coffee earlier.

She hoped she had something to make for dinner here because she had no plans to go out anywhere to eat. If she did, she'd just run into people and have to face the stares. She headed to the kitchen and rummaged through the cabinets. Not much here, but she'd make do with something.

She glanced at her watch. She still had to run over to the theater and lock up. She'd go after dark when hopefully no one would see her. She'd lock it up and come straight back home.

And maybe Gavin would come by once he heard she'd been looking for him. Or... maybe not. He might be too mad at her.

She dropped her head into her hands, wondering how all this had gotten so out of control.

CHAPTER 23

Miss Eleanor called Gavin early the next morning and asked him to meet her at Coastal Coffee. When he walked in, he quickly scanned the room to make sure Tori—no, he had to remember to call her *Victoria* now—wasn't there.

No sign of her. Good.

He headed over to Miss Eleanor's table and sat down. She motioned to the steaming cup of coffee already sitting on the table waiting for him. "Ordered that for you."

He nodded and took a sip.

"So, what did Miss Duran say when you talked to her?"

He stared down at his coffee, unwilling to meet her gaze. "I didn't talk to her."

"I thought you said you would," she said sharply.

"I was headed over to talk to her and then..." He paused and looked at Miss Eleanor. "I saw her talking to Cliff. They were deep in conversation."

"Whatever for?"

"I'm not totally certain..." Did he dare tell her his speculations? Though the words he'd heard had been fairly clear.

"Spill it. I can see from the look on your face you know something."

"I'm wondering if she and Cliff have some kind of deal. If she bought it only to sell it to Cliff. I heard them talking about an offer."

"She wouldn't," Eleanor insisted, then her frown deepened and doubt crept across her features. "I mean, she had to restore it back to how it was... but then, I guess she could sell to whoever she wanted to. I just didn't think someone would put that much money into it if they weren't going to keep it open."

"I wouldn't think so either. Unless Cliff made her an offer she can't refuse. And I don't know if this might have been her plan all along. Or maybe Cliff took advantage of her... ah... situation now and he's making her an offer.

Either way, I'm afraid the town might lose the theater."

"That can't happen." Miss Eleanor insisted by double-tapping the table.

"I don't know how we can stop her if that's her plan."

"I'll buy it back." Miss Eleanor bobbed her head emphatically, her wispy white hair bouncing with determination.

"Unless Cliff has the money to outbid you." Grim thoughts clung to his mind as he thought of the deep pockets Cliff seemed to possess these days. First the land at the end of the boardwalk. Now this.

She scowled. "That son of mine is always causing trouble. I'll talk to my lawyer and make an offer to her. See if I can stop all this."

He nodded. "I hope we can. It would be a shame to have it restored, have a grand opening, only to close again."

"I can just see Cliff converting it into a modern bistro or something equally frivolous. We need the theater."

"We do. And I'm sorry I didn't see this coming. I thought I knew Tori—Victoria—but obviously, I didn't."

"None of us did."

CHAPTER 24

Tori tried to talk to Gavin over the next few days, but no luck. He wouldn't answer the messages she left on his phone. She swung by The Bike Shop multiple times, hoping to catch him there. Each time Jonny said Gavin wasn't there, but the guilty look on Jonny's face confirmed that Gavin was avoiding her.

A constant stream of reporters besieged her. Bothering her at the theater, chasing her down when they spied her on the street. She'd chased away more reporters than she cared to count. Each one wanting an exclusive story. Each one wanting to be the one to break the news on when she might come back to New York City and return to Broadway. She never said a word to any of them.

And she would swear that in the last few days the people in town were even more mad at her, if that was even possible. The icy glares she got when she walked to the theater and passed anyone were filled with anger. She could feel their stares burning into her back as she walked by them. It was as if the whole town had turned against her.

She sat at her desk with the opening just days away, wondering if anyone would even show up for it. Would all the seats be empty in a collaborative effort to show her how angry they were for keeping her true identity a secret?

But she'd been trying to help the town. Get the theater back up and running. But now she just felt alone and misunderstood, with no chance to ever feel like a real part of the town. And if the opening failed? The theater failed? Then what was she going to do? Disappointment and despair clung to her every move, her every decision.

She looked up in surprise as Miss Eleanor strode into the room. "Here." Miss Eleanor dropped some papers on her desk. "I'm making an offer on the theater."

"Why?" She glanced down at the papers

and frowned, confused. "But why would you think I was selling the theater?"

"Selling it to Cliff. He made an offer didn't he?"

"Yes, but—"

Miss Eleanor cut her off with a wave of her hand. "I want it to stay a theater. Not get torn down for some monstrosity that Cliff would build, or turned into some ill-conceived place he thinks the town needs, but we don't." Miss Eleanor shook her head. "I thought better of you, Miss Duran. Thought you realized the historical significance of the theater for this town. I thought... Well, I was wrong. And if my offer isn't more than Cliff's, I can come up with some more money. But I'm hoping you'll accept this. For the good of the town."

She rose from her desk and walked slowly around it to stand in front of Miss Eleanor. "I don't won't your offer, don't accept it."

"Have you already sold it to Cliff?" A brief look of panic, quickly hidden, darted across the woman's face.

"No. I haven't sold it to Cliff. And I'm not selling it to you. I'm not selling it to anyone."

Miss Eleanor's eyes narrowed. "You aren't?"

"No, I love this theater. I want it to be a

success. I'd planned on staying here and managing it, but I'm not certain that's a viable plan anymore."

"Because?"

"Because it's obvious that no one in the town trusts me. It was hard enough to try and feel like I might—just might—begin to feel like part of the town. But now? People either stare at me or glare at me. And neither one is very welcoming."

"You did keep your true identity a secret from all of us."

She shifted uncomfortably under the woman's piercing gaze. She could no more tell Miss Eleanor the whole truth than she could tell Gavin. "I… I had my reasons," she said weakly.

Miss Eleanor gave her a long glance. "I see. Well, I assume they were good reasons?"

She hesitated. Were they good reasons? She knew they were. But just saying she'd grown tired of her fame, of Broadway, sounded lame even to her own ears. "They were. They are." She hoped she sounded confident.

Miss Eleanor paused and looked at her closely for a long moment before nodding once. "Then, okay. A woman is allowed to keep parts of her past a secret if she wishes."

Tori had the distinct feeling that Miss Eleanor was talking about herself as much as she was talking about Tori's choice to keep Victoria Duran a secret.

For a moment, she felt a brief bonding with the woman, so she decided to confess her fears. "I'm afraid we'll have our big grand opening and the seats will be empty. Or just a few people scattered around. If the opening fails, I'm afraid the theater just won't make it. I tried so hard, and all this work might have been for nothing."

"Hmph. Not if I can help it." Miss Eleanor shook her head. "And I think you should stand your ground. Stay here if you want. Or go if you need to. I'm just ashamed I acted like an idiot after seeing that article. That I didn't just come here and ask you to explain. Not that you had to give me the exact reason. Just assure me there was a good reason."

And just like that, Miss Eleanor was the first person in Magnolia to show her some grace. A weight lifted off her shoulders, and she felt like she could finally take a breath.

Miss Eleanor took Tori's hands in her own wrinkled ones and squeezed them. "I'll be here at the opening, front row, and so will a good crowd if I have anything to do with it."

A flutter of hope began to grow in her, easing the knot of anxiety that had been with her constantly over the last few weeks.

"But I will say one thing. I do think you need to talk to Gavin. He was surprised to hear the truth... and a bit hurt, I think. Hurt that you didn't at least share with him."

"He won't talk to me. Won't take my calls. Jonny always says he's gone when I stop by The Bike Shop."

"He's as big a fool as I am. We both should have known you had a good reason for keeping your past a secret. People in a small town often think we should know each other's business. But you know what? We shouldn't. People should be able to have some secrets. Especially if they don't hurt anyone."

Acceptance. She had one person in town on her side.

"And the people in town will come around. Or at least most of them will. They'll move on to some other bit of gossip."

"I guess Magnolia isn't that different from Broadway in that regard."

"I'm sure the gossip will die down there, too." Miss Eleanor dropped her hands and stepped back. "You go find Gavin and make him listen to you. Then… he'll do whatever he does. But you'll at least have tried to make him understand."

But how would he understand if she couldn't tell him the whole reason, the real reason she left Broadway to hide out on Magnolia Key?

Cliff walked into Coastal Coffee that afternoon, the bell over the door jingling merrily to announce his arrival. Beverly sucked in a sharp, startled breath at the sight of him. "We're closing, Cliff. Find somewhere else to eat."

He glanced at the hours posted on the door. "Says you're still open for forty-five minutes."

"Closing early." She glanced down at her clenched fists and slowly uncurled them, annoyed that he could get this kind of reaction out of her. *Any* reaction out of her.

"A guy can't even get a cup of coffee?" He tossed her one of his charming grins, the one she remembered so well.

But she was immune. "There are other places in town to get one."

"But you have the best coffee on the island."

"I do. But we're still closing." Why did he insist on coming around? Especially with their history. With the way he'd just disappeared from her life. After they'd planned a life *together.* But she'd made a life for herself. A good life. Without him. Look at her now. A successful businesswoman with no need for him or any man in her life. But especially not Cliff.

She folded her arms and turned her back on him. He reached out and touched her arm, but she shrugged his touch away.

"Don't be like that. I'm sorry. I was just a kid back then."

"So was I. A heartbroken one." Her words were filled with the bitterness she still felt, the old wounds still poking her.

"But that was in the past. You can't hold a grudge forever, can you?"

"I can." She turned back to face him. "And the rumor that you're trying to buy the theater only adds to my extreme dislike of you."

He scowled. "Okay, I admit, I tried to buy it. But Victoria wouldn't sell it to me."

"She wouldn't?" Now that surprised her. She figured after all that had happened, Tori would cut and run.

"No. She was afraid I'd tear it down."

"And was that your plan?" She cocked her head, watching his face closely to see if he would tell the truth.

"It was." He shrugged. "Going to build a modern hotel. The island needs at least one of them. And if I can get the town council on my side for the property at the end of the boardwalk, we'll have somewhere decent to stay there, too."

"We have plenty of charming places for people to stay. We don't need modern and new."

"Then the town will just die away."

"I don't think so, Cliff. This town is stronger than you think."

Maxine came striding out of the kitchen, her eyes flashing. "Cliff, what are you doing here?"

Beverly almost smiled at her friend's defensive, protective attitude. And would have if she wasn't so furious with Cliff.

"Just getting a cup of coffee," he said casually, implying he had every right to be here.

"I asked him to leave, but… he's not being very agreeable to the suggestion."

Maxine walked right up to him and shoved a finger at his chest. "Cliff, just go. Beverly

KAY CORRELL

doesn't want you here. And don't come back,
okay?" Her words came out fiercely protective.

He stared at Maxine for a moment, then
turned his gaze back to her. "I never can do
anything right in this town, can I?" With that,
he turned and strode out the door, letting it slam
behind him.

Beverly let out a deep breath, trying to calm
her racing heart.

"You okay?" Maxine looked at her closely,
concern in her eyes.

"I will be now that he's gone. Oh, and you
know that rumor that's swirling around town
that he's buying the theater from Tori and
tearing it down?"

"Yes?"

"Well, he's not. She turned him down." A
rush of gratitude toward Tori for standing up to
Cliff flowed through her.

"She did?" Maxine's eyes widened. "I
figured she'd sell to the highest bidder and head
back to Broadway."

"Guess not." Beverly shrugged. But she
wondered just what Tori's plans were now.

"Well, I feel better about going to opening
night with Dale now. I didn't want to support
her if she was selling the place."

"Right. And we should make sure the rumor of her selling dies and people show up for the opening, because we all want the theater to be a success, don't we?" They needed the whole town to rally behind Tori now.

"We do."

CHAPTER 25

Tori headed over to The Bike Shop. She asked for Gavin and Jonny blushed and stammered when he said Gavin wasn't there. Enough of this. She shook her head in frustration and strode toward the back of the shop, pushing aside the curtain to the door of their repair room. There was Gavin, his hands greasy, standing over an upturned bike.

His eyes widened in surprise, then narrowed in irritation. "Thought I told Jonny to say I wasn't here."

"He has been saying that. Each time I come by. But I didn't listen to him today."

Gavin sighed and turned back to the bike with a dismissive shrug. "Well, you should have. We don't have anything to say."

She walked up closer to him, stepping over scattered tools and parts, determined to make him listen. "But I think we do."

He set down the rag he was holding, making no attempt to wipe away the grease, and turned back to her. "No, we don't," he said, his words brittle with finality.

"So you're just never going to talk to me again? I never lied to you. I just didn't tell you every detail about my past. I bet you haven't told me everything about your past."

"I did. And I told you about Anna. And how I never wanted to be involved with someone that the media flocks to."

"I'm not like that. I walked away from all of that." She watched his face, hoping to see some crack in his stony expression.

"Really? Did you?" Gavin snapped. "How many reporters do you think have come to town in the last few days?"

"I haven't spoken to any of them except to ask them to leave," she insisted, her frustration mounting.

He pinned her with a fierce look. "I know you're selling the theater to Cliff and heading back to Broadway. Don't lie to me."

Exasperated, she stamped her foot. "Gavin,

I'm not lying. You're not listening to me. I was never selling it to Cliff. He wanted to buy it, but I turned him down."

"You did?" He looked skeptical. "How do I know I can believe you?"

"Because it's the truth. And I turned down Miss Eleanor's offer to buy it too. I want to stay here and run the theater. Make my life here. I want…" She took a deep breath, gathering her courage. "I want to stay here… with you. See what happens between us. I… I care about you." There, she'd laid her feelings bare. And she wanted to kiss him again, to hear him laugh, to share little tidbits about her day when she saw him in the evening. She wanted that and so much more.

He stood there silently watching her, then finally said, "I don't trust that you won't run back to the limelight. Leave. And I don't know why you couldn't tell me about your past. Why you hid it from me." His tone held the tiniest bit of hurt that he couldn't disguise.

"I didn't tell anyone about what I used to do. I just wanted to be Tori for a change. Have people like me for me, not for being an actress."

He crossed his arms, his expression

unreadable. "I'm not sure what you want me to say here."

"I want you to say you accept my apology. That you'll give us a chance. That everything will be okay." Her heart thundered, clinging to her last shred of hope.

"I'm sorry. That's not something I can give you. I'll accept your apology, but it won't make any difference. We can't be together. We can't."

"But, Gavin—"

He held up his hand. "No." He turned his back on her. "I have to get back to work."

She turned and walked out of the back room, across the concrete floor of the shop, and out into the sunlight. She wasn't sure what she'd expected. She had hidden who she was. And he'd plainly told her the other night on the beach that he would never date someone famous.

Tears tugged at the corners of her eyes, and she swiped them away. Maybe things would have been different if she had told him sooner who she was. Or if she could tell him the whole truth now. Then maybe he'd understand why she did what she did. But... she couldn't tell him or anyone. The producer of her last show had made sure of that.

She trudged down the sidewalk, the glare of the sun mocking each step as if asking what she had expected. A fresh start? That he actually cared about her? She should have known better.

She'd hoped that she could have another chance with Gavin. But he'd made it clear that wasn't going to happen now.

She went to the theater and climbed the front steps, entering the lobby where she was surrounded by the hum of excitement. She squared her shoulders, determined to put all this with Gavin behind her. She had a theater to run and the opening to focus on. The show must go on, she thought wryly. That was all that mattered now. This theater was all she had.

CHAPTER 26

Miss Eleanor came into The Bike Shop the morning of the theater's grand opening. He stifled a sigh, knowing he was in for another lecture. "Morning Miss Eleanor," he called out cheerfully.

"Don't paste that fake smile on your face, young man," she said, her sharp eyes missing nothing.

And it had been a really, *really* long time since someone had called him a young man.

"What's this nonsense that you and Tori aren't speaking? Did you even help her with the last-minute details of the opening?"

"Trust me, *Victoria* has everything covered."

She pinned him with a long, hard stared.

"*Tori* has given her heart and soul to restoring this theater. She's worked tirelessly. And look at all she accomplished. And she stood up to that fool son of mine when he offered her a ridiculous sum for the theater."

Miss Eleanor's impassioned defense of Tori made him shift uncomfortably. He knew Tori had put hours and hours into restoring the theater, and she'd done a remarkable job. But it didn't change the fact that they had gone their separate ways. At his insistence, but still.

He set down the wrench he'd been holding. "That doesn't really change things, though, does it? She lied to me."

"Did she? Or did she just not tell you everything about her past? You know, no one is obliged to tell everything they've done in the past. Some things are better left unsaid, unknown. And she must have had her reasons for not wanting people to know who she was."

"But—"

She cut him off. "Gavin Sloan, do not 'but' me. She's a hardworking, wonderful young woman."

He was fairly confident that Tori hadn't been called a young woman recently, either. He shoved the thought aside.

"I think you're foolish, clinging to some kind of grudge against her. You two worked great together and accomplished quite the feat by reopening the theater. It looks wonderful. Better than before. And she's got a show opening tonight." She came over to the counter and double-tapped it with one finger. "And you're coming tonight to show your support, aren't you?"

"I... I'm not sure."

"Gavin Sloan, you're better than that." She scowled at him, pivoted abruptly, and walked out of the shop.

He let out a long sigh, confusion swirling through him like a restless tide. Maybe he had been a bit too hard on her. He'd let his hurt feelings cloud his judgment, acting more from a place of wounded pride than anything. He'd been so surprised to learn she'd kept her past a secret from him. He'd thought he knew her so well. But as Miss Eleanor pointed out, Tori must have had her reasons for coming here as simply Tori Duran.

He stalked across the shop, grabbed a tire, and headed back to replace the flat on the bike he'd been working on. But even the methodical tasks of fixing the tires did little to quiet the conflicted thoughts racing around his mind. Nor did it help him make a decision about tonight. The right choice eluded him.

CHAPTER 27

Tori rushed around all day, making sure everything was ready for the opening. Checking ticket sales, making sure the lobby was sparkling and the concession stand was set to go. Keeping herself way too busy to think about Gavin. Mostly. But somehow he still managed to creep into her thoughts. He should have been here with her, sharing the excitement of opening night. And yet, here she was, alone.

She hurried home as evening approached and changed into a simple black dress and heels before returning to the theater, her nerves tied into a tight knot. Taking a moment to collect her thoughts in her office, she unlocked her desk drawer and pulled out the pendant she'd found. The desk light caught the gems, making them gleam as she traced her fingers over the design. She slipped the necklace on and fastened the clasp, comforted by the weight of it.

"Okay, it's just us. And I'm hoping you bring the theater good luck tonight. You can do that, can't you?" She touched the pendant again, hoping the heirloom could indeed make tonight magical.

She returned to the lobby and paced back and forth, glancing repeatedly at the time, nervously waiting for the doors to open. When they finally were, she held her breath, hoping people would come. Anyone. At first, just a few people entered. Then, to her extreme surprise and relief, people started streaming into the lobby. Some said hi to her, some didn't, but at least they were here.

She lifted her hand to the necklace again, feeling the delicately crafted magnolia under her fingertips. "Bring the show good luck," she whispered to it.

Beverly, Maxine, and Dale walked up to her with friendly smiles on their faces. A welcome sight. "Looks like a great turnout," Beverly said as she glanced around the bustling lobby.

"I'm... surprised. I thought that no one would come."

"Well, Miss Eleanor suggested that we all do. And she's right. Your past is no business of ours. You've done right by our theater and we're proud of you." Beverly gave her a hug, which she accepted gratefully.

"Yes, we are." Maxine nodded in agreement. "You've done a wonderful job. It's great to have the theater open again."

Dale looked at her closely for a moment, his eyes narrowing, his expression thoughtful. Then he snapped his fingers. "I know where I've seen it before. The pendant. It was in a stack of photos in a box at my shop. Old photos from the theater. One of the actresses was wearing it. He frowned for a moment. "It was from a scene from Old Man River. I'm almost certain."

"Was a Vera Whitmore wearing it?"

Dale nodded. "Yes, that was it."

"I have a program framed over there on the wall. She was a star in the show."

"Vera *Whitmore?* One of Miss Eleanor's relatives?" Beverly's eyes widened.

"She was my great-aunt." Miss Eleanor walked up to them, staring at the pendant hanging around her neck.

"She was?" Tori touched the pendant, feeling the weight of history in it.

"I hadn't seen that in years until you showed me it at Coastal Coffee. I thought it was… lost." Miss Eleanor's voice cracked just slightly with the last word. "I was so surprised to see it again. I should have told you it was Aunt Vera's. She was just always so secretive about it. Although, I know it meant a lot to her."

Dale frowned. "I think there was some actual write-up about this piece of jewelry. I'm just sure I saw something. I'll have to go back and do some research. I'll see what I can find out."

"Thank you." Tori gave him an appreciative smile.

Miss Eleanor's eyes filled with sadness as she continued to stare at the necklace.

Tori reached up to unhook it. "Then you should have this. It's your family's."

"No, dear. That pendant belongs to the theater, not me." Miss Eleanor put on a smile that didn't erase the sadness in her eyes. "Anyway, Miss Duran, break a leg. I'm sure the opening will be a huge success."

"Thank you. I hope so."

Miss Eleanor gave a small wave, still lost in her memories, and turned to make her way into the theater.

Beverly turned to Maxine. "I knew Miss Eleanor recognized it when she saw it at the cafe. I'm glad she told us about it now."

Dale gestured to the theater doors. "So, should we go in?"

"Yes. And let Tori get back to her work," Maxine agreed, giving Tori a supportive smile.

She returned the smile, grateful for their support. She stood in the lobby, greeting people and scanning the crowd, looking for Gavin. But there was no sign of him, and her heart sank a little at his absence.

With a quiet sigh, she turned and headed backstage to see if she could be any help there. It was better than standing in the lobby hopelessly waiting for something that was never going to happen.

The organized chaos of the dressing room welcomed her with a familiar embrace. This was her element, the world she knew best. Tonight was too important to be distracted by personal disappointments.

Tori paced back and forth backstage, listening to every word of the play. She held her breath when the lead actress tripped over her lines in a pivotal scene, but luckily another actor improvised smoothly, covering for her. She let out her breath, realizing that no one in the audience was any the wiser.

The lighting technician was spot on, each spotlight and floodlight carefully angled to highlight the actors exactly as planned. Not a squeak or pop from the sound system. The actors' voices rang clearly throughout the theater.

Before she knew it, the final act was drawing to a close. She let out a deep breath of relief. Soon the sound of thunderous applause filled the theater. The star of the show motioned for her to come out on stage. She hung back for a moment until another actress came over and grabbed her hand, dragging her onto the stage.

The cheering grew even louder, and she basked in the familiar sound of applause as tears gathered in her eyes. She'd done it. After all the struggles and setbacks, the beloved theater was back open, and the show was a success.

As the applause died down, she walked up to where a mic would pick up her words. "I want to thank all of you for coming tonight. For supporting our efforts to open the theater again and experience the magic of a live performance. I thank you from the bottom of my heart."

Applause started up, and she heard someone call out from the back of the theater. "Way to go, Tori. You did it."

Someone else called out, "Yay, Tori. Bravo!"

Happiness swelled through her at their support and appreciation. She waved warmly to the audience and headed off stage with the cast, her eyes glistening. Backstage, the cast milled around, trading hugs and laughter. Someone popped open a bottle of champagne.

Her happiness was only dimmed by not being able to share the opening with Gavin. She had hoped he'd be here at her side, sharing the moment, seeing the result of all their hard work. They were no longer together, but a part of her still yearned for his support on this momentous night.

"Aunt Victoria?"

She whirled around at the sound of Chloe's voice, breaking her from her wistful thoughts. A smile spread across her face as she hurried over to embrace her niece.

"Chloe." She hugged her tightly. And then, looking over Chloe's shoulder, she saw him.

Gavin. Standing there watching her. A bouquet of flowers in his hands.

She stepped back, surprise flashing through her, but turned her gaze back to Chloe. "You're here," she said, her voice thick with emotion.

"I wouldn't have missed it. I think it's a lovely thing you've done restoring the theater."

Pride swept through her at her niece's compliment. She *had* restored the theater back to its glory. It was alive again, just like it should be.

"And Aunt Victoria, I found out."

She tensed, and a trill of panic started rising inside her. "Found out what?" she asked, trying to keep her voice steady and calm.

"I know why you left. The theater community is a tight-knit group. I know the producers of your last show stole the script from Christopher Snow. Everyone knows by now, I imagine, because I leaked the news to the media this morning."

She gasped. "Oh, no, you shouldn't have done that." All her efforts to protect her niece, and now Chloe did this, risking everything.

"Well, I also heard you kept it a secret because they threatened to blacklist me from the stage if you told anyone."

"But now... don't you see? They will. You shouldn't have said anything. I feel guilty enough that I kept it quiet. But I had to. You have a brilliant future on the stage."

Chloe set her jaw stubbornly. "I'm not going to be the reason that you leave the stage or a young playwright gets screwed over. And I heard that Christopher Snow had an anonymous donor who backed his new play. You wouldn't have any idea who that was, would you?" Chloe's eyes twinkled knowingly. "I bet I do."

Despite herself, she smiled slightly. "I was just trying to make things right."

"Now that the story is breaking, I've heard that your former producer will be forced to pay Christopher what he's due. And I heard that very same producer is being removed from his current production."

"Really?" Relief washed over her. Christopher was finally getting what he was owed. He'd get justice.

Chloe hugged her again, her eyes shining with affection. "And don't you see? Now you can come back to Broadway. Act again. I've missed having you in New York City."

Tori looked long at her niece. Chloe was right. She could easily go back to Broadway now. She was sure she could get another acting part. But she might have to dye her hair back to red, she thought wryly.

Gavin was still staring at her, flowers in hand.

She reached out and took Chloe's hand. "No, sweetie. I'm not coming back. Not now. Not in the future. I'm done with stage life. I've found a new life here on Magnolia Key. One I love. A charming little town I love." She glanced over at Gavin. "And people I… I care about."

Her niece threw her arms around her, hugging her tightly. "Then this is where you should stay. I will say, I've never seen you happier, more glowing than when you came out after the show and thanked the audience."

"I promise I'll come catch your show soon."

"I'd like that." Chloe turned to Gavin. "I know I butted in right when you were getting ready to give those flowers to Aunt Victoria. And if you're the one she was saying she cares about? Don't mess it up. She's a special lady."

Chloe turned back to her and kissed her cheek. "Got to run. Have to get back to New York for tomorrow's performance. I love you."

"Love you too, sweetheart."

Chloe disappeared into the crowd, and

Gavin walked over, handing her the flowers. "These are for you."

She took them and stared down at them, focusing on their delicate petals, her heart beating wildly.

"Tori, I'm so sorry," Gavin said, his voice thick with regret. "I should have known you had a good reason for keeping your past in the past. And you did. You were protecting your niece."

She nodded slowly, her eyes still fixated on the flowers as she took in his words.

"You are a truly wonderful person and I'm a fool."

With that, her lips curved up in a smile, and she looked up and reached out to touch his face. "As long as you're my fool, I'm good with that."

He grinned and stepped forward, pulling her into his arms, crushing the flowers. But she didn't care about the flowers. Didn't care who was watching them. All she cared about in that moment was being back in Gavin's arms, where she belonged.

CHAPTER 28

Time flew by in a flurry of activity. Each night people streamed into the theater and the show closed to thunderous applause. The thrill of the performances never waned, and the roar of applause that followed the final curtain call each night filled Tori's heart with such joy. Magnolia Theater was back.

The show's two-week run concluded with the bittersweet final show. Tori had seen Gavin almost every night. But now, with the successful opening show behind them, they had time to spend together, away from the theater.

Hand-in-hand they headed out to the quiet end of the beach, their steps measured and in perfect rhythm. Finally, finally, they were falling in sync with each other.

He looked down at her as they walked in comfortable silence. "Are you relieved to have your first production behind you?"

"I am. And a bit sad. It was so special. And I'm just so pleased at how well it turned out and how well it was received."

"You did a wonderful job."

Her cheeks flushed at this praise. "*We* did a wonderful job. I know I might have balked at some of your suggestions, and you were annoyingly right at times..." She teased him. "But I really loved working with you."

He paused and lightly touched her cheek. "And I enjoyed working with you. It was a very special time, Tori Duran."

She savored the warmth of his touch, her heart full of happiness and looking forward to so much more for the theater. "I have one more play scheduled, and soon we can have a regular schedule and also use the theater for town events. And do some productions with local actors. Just like they used to do when I was young. Oh, and the principal has already asked for it for high school graduation. And a young woman whose mother used to perform here in the town productions wants to hold a small wedding at the theater. They're going to get married on stage. Her mother is thrilled."

"Sounds like Magnolia Theater is back up and running. Just what this town needed."

"It's what I needed." She gave his hand another grateful squeeze as they continued down the path.

They reached the beach and walked across it, their feet sinking into the cool, powdery sand. As they reached the water's edge, they stood and let the foamy edge of the waves splash up over their feet before it rushed back out to sea. She could stand like this forever with Gavin. Stand here at the edge of the world where time stood still. The vast ocean stretched before her, reminding her how tiny they were in the scheme of things, and yet she felt infinite with Gavin at her side. Capable of anything. Ready for anything.

He looked down at her, his eyes filled with an emotion so strong it took her breath away. "You know something, Tori Duran?"

"What?" Her heart somersaulted from just seeing the look in his eyes. One she'd never seen there before.

His eyes never left hers as he spoke. "I love you."

Her heart recovered from the somersault just in time to zig-zag through her chest. "You do?"

"I do." He leaned down and brushed his lips against hers in a gentle, lingering kiss. She melted into his embrace.

When he finally pulled back, she looked directly into his eyes. "That's a good thing. A good thing you love me. Because you see, I love you too."

He broke into a wide grin. "And look at us. In sync now."

"Yes, we are." She reached up and touched his face, drawing a line across his cheek. The sun slipped below the horizon as she stood there, wrapped up in his arms as they watched the brilliant display before them. The moon rose like a spotlight over the waves, bathing them in its silvery light.

Peace settled over her, and she knew two things for certain: Magnolia Key was where she belonged, and her heart was Gavin's.

I hope you enjoyed Tori and Gavin's story. Are you ready for book three in the series? Coastal

Candlelight is Amanda's story. She's taking a break from her hectic life in the city and books a vacation rental on Magnolia Key—a place she'd visited with her parents. There she meets Connor, a reclusive woodworker. He wants nothing to do with the woman renting the cottage next to his. But fate has other plans for them...

Try Coastal Candlelight coming Fall of 2024. As always, I appreciate each of you and hope you're enjoying the Magnolia Key series.

Kay

ALSO BY KAY CORRELL

COMFORT CROSSING ~ THE SERIES

The Shop on Main - Book One

The Memory Box - Book Two

The Christmas Cottage - A Holiday Novella
(Book 2.5)

The Letter - Book Three

The Christmas Scarf - A Holiday Novella (Book 3.5)

The Magnolia Cafe - Book Four

The Unexpected Wedding - Book Five

The Wedding in the Grove (crossover short story
between series - Josephine and Paul from The Letter.)

LIGHTHOUSE POINT ~ THE SERIES

Wish Upon a Shell - Book One

Wedding on the Beach - Book Two

Love at the Lighthouse - Book Three

Cottage near the Point - Book Four

Return to the Island - Book Five

Bungalow by the Bay - Book Six

Christmas Comes to Lighthouse Point - Book Seven

CHARMING INN ~ Return to Lighthouse Point

One Simple Wish - Book One

Two of a Kind - Book Two

Three Little Things - Book Three

Four Short Weeks - Book Four

Five Years or So - Book Five

Six Hours Away - Book Six

Charming Christmas - Book Seven

SWEET RIVER ~ THE SERIES

A Dream to Believe in - Book One

A Memory to Cherish - Book Two

A Song to Remember - Book Three

A Time to Forgive - Book Four

A Summer of Secrets - Book Five

A Moment in the Moonlight - Book Six

MOONBEAM BAY ~ THE SERIES

The Parker Women - Book One

The Parker Cafe - Book Two

A Heather Parker Original - Book Three

The Parker Family Secret - Book Four

Grace Parker's Peach Pie - Book Five

The Perks of Being a Parker - Book Six

BLUE HERON COTTAGES ~ THE SERIES

Memories of the Beach - Book One

Walks along the Shore - Book Two

Bookshop near the Coast - Book Three

Restaurant on the Wharf - Book Four

Lilacs by the Sea - Book Five

Flower Shop on Magnolia - Book Six

Christmas by the Bay - Book Seven

Sea Glass from the Past - Book Eight

MAGNOLIA KEY ~ THE SERIES

Saltwater Sunrise - Book One

Encore Echoes - Book Two

Coastal Candlelight - Book Three

Tidal Treasures - Book Four

And more to come!

WIND CHIME BEACH ~ A stand-alone novel

INDIGO BAY ~

Sweet Days by the Bay - Kay's complete collection of stories in the Indigo Bay series

ABOUT THE AUTHOR

Kay Correll is a USA Today bestselling author of sweet, heartwarming stories that are a cross between women's fiction and contemporary romance. She is known for her charming small towns, quirky townsfolk, and the enduring strong friendships between the women in her books.

Kay splits her time between the southwest coast of Florida and the Midwest of the U.S. and can often be found out and about with her camera, taking a myriad of photographs, often incorporating them into her book covers. When not lost in her writing or photography, she can be found spending time with her ever-supportive husband, knitting, or playing with her puppies - a cavalier who is too cute for his own good and a naughty but adorable Australian shepherd. Their five boys are all grown now and while she misses the rowdy boy-noise chaos, she is thoroughly enjoying her empty nest years.

Learn more about Kay and her books at
kaycorrell.com

While you're there, sign up for her newsletter to
hear about new releases, sales, and giveaways.

WHERE TO FIND ME:
My shop: shop.kaycorrell.com
My author website: kaycorrell.com
authorcontact@kaycorrell.com

Join my Facebook Reader Group. We have lots
of fun and you'll hear about sales and new
releases first!
www.facebook.com/groups/KayCorrell/

I love to hear from my readers. Feel free to
contact me at authorcontact@kaycorrell.com

facebook.com/KayCorrellAuthor

instagram.com/kaycorrell

pinterest.com/kaycorrellauthor

amazon.com/author/kaycorrell

bookbub.com/authors/kay-correll

Made in the USA
Columbia, SC
07 August 2024

40123597R00164